That Church Life 3

Teresa B. Howell

Praise for That Church Life Series

That Church Life

Teresa B. Howell's "That Church Life" spines a tale of drama, suspense, romance and tragedy that invites readers to explore the universal intrigue of what lies as the core of the good and not so good realities in the church.
As seen in Huff Post

That Church Life is surprising, fast paced, and honest. I had a completely different idea of what to expect than how the story ended up being. It begins in the heart of the action as Missy is processing what happened. Everything follows her frame of thought as she goes through shock and confusion. The story felt cinematic in the best way with the quick pace, the action, and the dramatic elements. Teresa B. Howell finds the perfect balance. That Church Life has a lesson underneath of finding guidance and strength through any obstacle, and of friendship. A must-read!
Sherri Fulmer Moorer-Reader's favorite

A great story full of drama, secrets and what is going to happen next with a little romance mixed in. This was a very enjoyable story line, and a very interesting read. Not the normal Christian fiction like I'm used to. The characters were extremely flawed and made mistakes, but did attempt to do right, as well as repent and ask for forgiveness. The author also tackled issues not often talked about in regard to Christians. I can't wait to read book 2 in the series.
Shannon Harper-Reviewer

This is the story of three lifelong girlfriend, who were raised in the church to do right, but life gets in the way and the rest, as they say…is history.
Diamonds Literary World

That Church Life 2

Author Teresa B. Howell is another example of authors who get better with each story. That Church Life 2 takes us into the lives of Missy, Michelle and Natalia and reminds us that just because you believe in God doesn't mean you're immune from the troubles of the world.

Like us all these three have to battle against their own decisions and fight hard for their faith if they want to survive both physically and spiritually. Is it easy for them? Not at all! But what they discover is that they don't have to go through their challenges and difficulties alone.

Each girl has their secrets they have been keeping, their own shame that has been keeping them closed off from others and even from God. Can they overcome it and realize where real help lies? Entertaining and inspiring, That Church Life 2 is a reminder that being "saved" and safe doesn't mean you're immune from life's troubles. You're just more prepared for them if you accept and embrace God's help.

Conversations Magazine-Cyrus Webb

That Church Life 3 © 2017 Teresa B. Howell
ISBN: 978-0-9977732-4-8

This is a work of fiction. Names, characters, places, and incidents are a product of the author's imagination or used fictitiously and are not to be construed as real. Any resemblance to actual events, places, organizations, or persons living or dead is entirely coincidental.

All scripture quotations, unless otherwise indicated, are taken from the Holy Bible: New International Version (NIV) © 1973, 1978, 1984 by International Bible Society. Used by permission. All rights reserved.

Independent Self-Published through Walking in Victory Int. LLC. P.O. Box 15171 Durham, NC 27704 Printed in the USA Copyright © 2017 Teresa B. Howell

ISBN: 978-0-9977732-4-8

ACKNOWLEDGMENTS

Thank you to my husband, Calvin William Howell III. You pushed me to complete each and every book. Your words of encouragement helped the flow of the pen.

Thanks to all my readers for your continued support and awesome feedback.

Thanks to Jaqueline Thomas, Rhonda McKnight, and Victoria Christopher Murray for mentorship and training throughout my writing journey.

Thanks to the Victorious Ladies Reading Book Club for always encouraging me to finish!

Thanks to my sister scribe, Lachelle Weaver the author of Sister Surrogate and Christmas Past. A true Bull City Queen that wasn't going to allow me to quit.

Extended thanks to the Ellis, Richardson, Shaw, Howard, Howell, and Crawford family.

Teresa B. Howell

SPECIAL DEDICATION

This book is dedicated to my mother, Helen Jean Richardson Ellis, Era Bell Ellis, Eyvonne Woods, and Jessie Richardson. Rest in Heaven.

PREVIOUSLY IN THAT CHURCH LIFE...

The two-story church building that once stood tall on RTP Parkway had perished. I cried, watching the flames tower beyond the roof. It took hours upon hours to put the fire completely out. With all the manpower of firemen leaning in on tall ladders surrounding the building, the flames were hard to tame.

I screamed loudly, looking up into the clouds. "Why God? Why?"

Earlier that day, Olivia Wallace, Missy's biological mother, pulled up to the church grounds, leaping out of a 1981 red Ford truck with red gasoline cans, and bags of paper. She walked to the back of the vehicle, pulling out two more cans full of petroleum to add to her bountiful collection.

"What is she doing?" I asked, watching her from the window inside the church.

I could smell the gasoline lingering throughout. I yelled out the window at the top of my lungs, "You are the craziest woman on earth. You know that, Liv? Put that gas down before you blow up the place."

"Won't happen today, Henry. No money, no church."

"Have you lost your mind, woman? You know this is my mama's church. You destructive whoremonger, you."

Once I noticed she wasn't listening, I cleared the building as we were in the middle of noonday prayer. Five of the guards ran down the hall, frantically emptying every room and shouting, "Let's go, people. Noonday prayer is over. Let's go. Everyone out."

I made it to the walkway, coughing deeply from all the smoke. I watched Olivia pour every drop of liquid into the garden beds that surrounded the windows. She talked out loud to herself, walking back and forth, and putting the emptied cans back onto the truck.

"I don't know who told them that I was just going to go away without my money. They make me do things," she said, walking back to the flower beds and bunching up paper.

She reached into her pocket and pulled out a cigarette lighter. The pieces of paper quickly attached to the flames as she threw them down into every flower bed that surrounded the building. Lighting up the pieces of paper seemed to give her joy.

"Olivia, stop. What are you doing? Lord, help us, Jesus." I threw up my hands in desperation and then bent down, touching my knees, out of breath. "My arthritis can't take all of this. Don't do this to us. I will give you the money. Please. Don't do this," I howled in pain.

She continued talking to her group of imaginary friends and was totally lost in her imagination. She was in a zone that only one hundred thousand dollars could get her out of.

"They got me fighting folks, threatening folks, and now burning up property. All that man had to do was give me my money."

She bent down, jumbling up more paper, leaves and bark, decorating the flower beds evenly. The flames inched slowly up the bricks as she plopped down more items one by one. She flicked her lighter again, with her other hand placed on her tiny hips.

Once the inferno circled around the building, I yanked her from her duties and pulled her onto the grass. She looked at me with dull eyes.

"Look at those flames, sweet thang."

———

Days Later...

ı Yellow tape circled the 6,500-square-foot building. Signs that said private property stuck high in the muddy grass and were visible from the busy street. The dawn of the morning allowed the sun to crack into the surface of the sky, showing a tinge of light.

Although the building had been tarnished, the center frame of the structure had been saved. There was still access to offices and the dining hall with light treading across the broken glass from the windows.

Olivia Wallace tiptoed into the building with her brother in search of the safe that was tucked away in the pastor's study. They carried flashlights, rubber gloves, and rubber shoe coverings, not wanting to leave any form of evidence. They stumbled, jerked, and rocked around the cement foundation that was once a linoleum floor.

"We got to get that safe, Larry. He had one-hundred-dollar bills stacked all in that thing."

Larry moved around like a professional thief, maneuvering

his body so he wouldn't bump against any of the objects that flew off the office shelves from the fire.

"Liv, I shole' hope you're telling the truth about this one. I could use the cash." He rubbed his fingers together, anticipating the thought of being loaded with the church's money. He carried a large tool bag on his back filled with a shovel, hammer, and pliers. He didn't know how to crack a safe, but he was gonna do whatever it took to make it happen.

"It was over here in this area." Olivia felt her way, looking down at the floor.

"Sis. Look...I think that's it over there."

In the corner of the room was the black mini-safe.

They pried, banged, and pounced on the top and side of it with the tools. After several minutes of banging the door, the safe cracked open. They jumped up and down, excited about finding the mystery jackpot.

"You did it this time, Liv. I'll be darn. We're about to come up from the gutter and into the penthouse."

Larry danced around, singing, "Just Got Paid" by Johnny Kemp. He pulled out a pair of safety glasses from his bag, clearing all the residue off the door frame. As he inched closer to pull the door outward, there was a brown paper bag placed in the center.

"That's it. *That's it*," Olivia screamed. She reached her hands in and pulled out several plastic grocery bags. "It must be at the bottom."

"It better be." Her brother looked down, peeping in the bag.

She had gotten to the last piece of plastic that was left inside the paper bag. It had a note stuck down with glue.

She pulled it out and read it aloud:

This is what my God can do. He can tell me to go and get my money immediately after a fire, just so I can keep all of it away from you.

From the Pastor that don't owe you jack!

Olivia slumped over, howling with her raspy voice, "This man has cursed me. I know he has. There is no way I can be so unlucky." She kicked and screamed, banging her foot hard on the safe. Olivia grabbed it, wincing as it throbbed in sheer agony.

Her brother shook his head and put all his tools back into his bag. "I guess that is what happens when you don't have God on your side. Looks like these folks got God, Jesus, the Holy Spirit and all of heaven protecting them."

They exited the building with only the tool bag they entered in with...

PROLOGUE

Pastor Henry Cepheus Jones sat in his wooden rocking chair on his colonial-style front porch as his mind wandered. He became one with nature for a split second. He looked around at the massive yard full of oak trees, daffodils and sunflowers towering beside him, while appreciating God's splendor.

All he could think with the hefty breeze slapping him across his face was *church*. He had come to realize that church was his life and even if he wanted to walk away, he didn't have the education or skill set to do anything else. Church was all he knew. Ultimately, he never imagined taking the oath of pastor would be so challenging.

Some days more than others, he found joy in seeing souls saved, people leaving out of church with a snippet of hope and love being shared, Sunday after Sunday. However, he had trials on every hand while dealing with the murder of Tommy Lee Davis, the burning of his church, Mt. Zion, and now the primary caregiver of Michelle Hank's baby, Micah. The more he tried to get himself together, the more something drastic would happen. He was now questioning his calling, and on some days, he even questioned God.

"Is ministry still for me? Should I just leave ministry all together?" he pondered, rocking back and forth.

Biblical verses crossed his mind while he scratched his head and swatted away the flies around him.

The Bible says, for every struggle, God will provide a way out. I need a way out today, Lord.

He presumed Missy becoming pastor was going to be his way out. He thought by giving her full reign to pastor, he would be only in the shadows, breaking free to a nice hideaway or exotic island. But, Missy was barely making it with her walk with Christ. He realized she was worse off than he, with bouts of anxiety and a lingering past of domestic violence.

' He shook his head, trying to recall how he ended up in this leadership role in the first place. He sat back, drowning deep into his thoughts. Flashes of his childhood scrolled across his brain.

Earline "Big Mama" Jones, along with God, had a plan for my life. By the age of ten, I was the only child out of three children allowed to recite prayer at the dinner table. I would get so caught up in my future calling that my brothers and I played church every day after school. I practiced the role of preacher of course, pacing the floor, talking with my hands and making hacking noises, while the other two played the tambourine and washboard. We imitated a church service very well, mimicking church members' facial expressions, testimonies, and holy dances. At times, we called ourselves getting "high in the spirit" as we maneuvered around the living room.

Big Mama laughed each time she walked by us while going in and out of the kitchen, preparing her country-styled meal. She waltzed by every few minutes, staring at us in her polka dot house dress and screaming, "You better preach, boy!"

She pumped us up, throwing her hands in the air full of excitement like a Dallas Cowboy cheerleader. The more we praised God, the deeper the hack in my voice became. I stomped around for hours with my celery stick microphone as sweat dripped down my tiny nose. I never got tired of praising God during play time or a real-life church service.

Late at night, Big Mama would tip into our room, wearing fluffy house slippers and a pair of underwear she used as a night cap hanging over her head. She would grab my little hand, dragging me into the living room for pep talks. I'd climb up on the high-seated, plastic covered sofa as Big Mama whispered softly in my ear.

"Son, God has a strong pull on your life. You will preach to the masses one day. People from all walks of life will cling to you because of what God has put inside of you." Her index finger shook wildly in front of my face. I would nod in agreement, blinking my eyes and laying sideways on her handmade, checkered, colorful quilt I dragged on the floor everywhere I went inside our home.

í"Yes, Ma'am."

Big Mama would get excited talking about God and her voice would become deep in between words. It was as if she couldn't turn the preaching dial off. Her plump dark lips would move nonstop while she emphasized my future destiny as pastor.

"When you become a preacher, always give God's word with passion and truth. Be a righteous man, son."

"Yes, Ma'am," I responded, wiping my sleepy eyes clean from the mucus that formulated around them.

"You're exactly what the people of God need."

I nodded in agreement.

"And, you know what else, son?" She poked me in my side to ensure that I was still listening.

"What?"

"When you remain in God's presence, the people of God will always stick by your side."

Her lengthy speeches ended with her soft hands brushing against my chubby cheeks. Eventually, I would find myself leaning into her full-figured hips and oversized chest, holding her tightly.

"I love you, Mama, and I'm ready to give God's word."

Her deep smile signified she was pleased with my obedience as she hugged back even tighter.

"Now, that's a Godly child. I love you too, my lil' preacher man. And, Henry Cepheus?"

"Yes, Mama?"

"When I leave this world, stand tall as the church leader. Dare to be different and let God use you, hear?"

Starry-eyed at her confidence in me, I'd grinned widely. "Yes, Ma'am."

"Your brothers better not even think about coming between you and God 'cause you, my dear, are the chosen one."

I looked up with a serious face, holding back emotion. "Yes, Ma'am. I promise, I won't let you or God down."

He rocked back and forth, now remembering why he became all about *That Church Life* and curved his mouth with a smile. Even in the midst of turmoil, God protected him. He was chosen and anointed to carry the preacher's torch until death parted him from it. He was committed to God and after going back in time, he realized he couldn't turn back now. Preaching equaled everything.

He inhaled deeply.

He felt better now about his current situation, blinking back at the sunflowers that seemed to be watching him as they stood up higher from the shift of wind. It was his little sign from heaven that reassured him, God was going to fix it *all*.

PART I

· *I'M A SOLDIER IN THE ARMY OF THE LORD.*

"Let us as Paul did, continue to press on through life."
Phil. 3:12

PASTOR JONES

CHAPTER 1

Five months after the fire...

It's said that people handle death differently. Some might grieve consistently, finding it difficult to move on, while others move forward with ease, realizing that death is part of the inevitable life cycle. I'm part of the first group of individuals finding it hard to live without Earline "Big Mama" Jones.

It was sixteen years ago on this day that "Big Mama" went home to be with the Lord, but my heart ached this early Sunday morning as if she just left me yesterday. I stood in front of the medium-sized podium, hitting my designer cufflinks against the cherry wood finish. I remained distinguished in my black Armani suit with matching shoes, despite how I felt. I could hear Big Mama say, *"If you look good, you feel good,"* as I popped my collar and cleared my throat.

I grabbed my Bible, fidgeting with the tassel that laid between the pages. I had to finagle my way through this service the best way I knew how. All I could do was stand upright and accept the waves of grief that floated around my heart, yet carry on with the service.

"Now, it's offering time," I mumbled in disgust.

ʳThe audience stood up, following the ushers' command of moving to the left. The deacons stood in the front of the church, posed like military soldiers holding up deep wicker baskets high in the air. As brown envelopes, green bills, and coins were thrown into the basket, the choir swayed back and forth to the beat of, "There's No God Like Our God."

The temporary space of worship wasn't even one-fourth the size of the old, long-standing Mt. Zion building. After the fire, finding a place within the city limits was crucial. The community center on Fayetteville Street was a perfect fit.

Only three hundred people could fit into the one-story, 1,800-square-foot community building. We made sure the center was back in tip-top shape after each service and ready for its weekly bridal showers, birthday parties, and bar mitzvahs. The other 2,600 members watched service on TCT, Word Network, Facebook Live, or Periscope.

I gazed around the room, straightening my face and watching individuals tightly squeeze their bodies back into each row of chairs. My thoughts shifted back and forth from Mama's death, to taking money from the church, paying off my wrongs, and then the awful day of the fire. Everything was on my mind, but the word of God.

Nevertheless, I had to give today's word anyway, since Missy was out of town. I had to shake these thoughts...fast.

The last offering giver walked around, and the deacons shouted, "Thank you for your liberal giving."

I cleared my throat without hesitation, leaning into the microphone. "Now, it's time for the word. Let us pray."

The audience stood up, venerating the prayer to the Almighty as music played softly in the background. The melodic tone resembled soothing elevator music. I tried not to stammer over my words and ended the prayer with, "In Jesus's name we pray...Amen."

"Amen," the congregation reeled back.

I flipped through the new King James version, finding a potent scripture in Psalms. I cracked a smile, gazing up at the crowd, now full of confidence. The fiery word I was about to spit into the mic was going to make everything alright. When I finished my sermon titled, "A Way Maker," I leaned forward, raising both hands in reverence. My powerful and final words flew out of my mouth easily. My burdens were getting light and my sadness was being dissolved.

"The word of God for the people of God. Amen?"

I inched back from the microphone, taking a deep breath

and waiting for a high time in the Lord to begin with hand clapping, feet stomping, and tongue talking. But instead, I received a soft, "Amen," with unmoving bodies and a few echoing coughs.

There wasn't a clap, or a hallelujah heard from anyone. The congregation remained seated in silence with their reflections bouncing off my thick reading glasses. Funeral fans swished rapidly from side to side. It was the only detection of life. Some of the faces in front of me were scrunched up, while others from a distance seemed to be fiddling with their cell phones.

It was such an awkward moment, expecting one thing and getting something totally different from the crowd. My lips parted, not knowing what to do next. I needed to see a sprinkle of love in their eyes or even a grin of confirmation. But instead, they looked as if they were waiting for my execution.

Did my sermon do anything for their souls?

Did I still have my preaching gift or not?

The longer I stood in silence, the deeper their frowns. They didn't scare me though. With God in the midst, I was down for whatever.

What was happening in the house of God that I wasn't aware of?

PASTOR JONES

CHAPTER 2

In the midst of me trying to figure it all out, a sudden outburst broke loose, moving their vicious eyes to the front row. Mother Shirley Smithfield, the oldest member of the church was having her usual bouts of chest pain. The emotions of the congregation ran high when the camera man zoomed in on her manly hands clutching her oversized chest. She leaned over into the middle of the aisle as if she was about to mimic the comedian Redd Foxx's famous lines from *Sanford and Son*. *"This is the big one, Elizabeth. I'm coming to join you, honey."*

Her flowered balloon dress flapped over her chair, showing her big, ham hock legs and swollen ankles. Her orthopedic shoes were pointed straight up, exposing large toe corns through the hard leather sole. Her face glistened with sweat while her glasses flung off her face, slamming against the podium.

I dropped the microphone, no longer concerned about the

services and rushed to her side. I recognized my *"suddenly"* experience from God as it came crashing down shifting their eyes from me. They stopped examining my weary soul and focused on Mother's desperate cry.

"Come on, Mother, breathe. Father God, we need you, Lord, right now." The crowd stood up, swaying peacefully and praying silently.

Seconds later, Mother's lips twitched from side to side as she reached out to touch my hand, formulating her words slowly.

"I'm gonna be alright, Passuh. The spirit of the Lord is in this place." Her eyes fluttered as she continued, "I guess I just got excited, along with a little pinch of acid reflux." She took short breaths, struggling to push her words out. "But, it's okay, son. Jesus got me."

I gave a partial smile, sucking back the tears that tried to sneak out of the corner of my eyes. "Glad to hear, Mother, because I need you here with me."

She was a sweet and gentle soul when she wanted to be. However, other folks in the church would beg to differ. I reached back, rubbing her palms gently for a tinge of support. "It's alright, Mother. It's alright."

Spots of love poured from her eyes as she gripped my left hand tightly. Although my daughter, Missy, was my only blood relative attending the church, Mother was considered part of my family too. No matter the sin, she always forgave me just as fast as God did.

I pounced my free hand on Mother's shoulder pad. The church nurse walked over, patting her forehead with a colorful handkerchief.

"Mother, I think we need to call the paramedics. I know you probably don't want me to do that. But, you need to get checked out right now."

"Nah-uh. Leave me be," she screeched.

"Mother, now is not the time to be stubborn."

"You heard what I said, Cepheus," she demanded with one eye opened and one eye closed.

Her voice was in my head from childhood. *"Listen to me when I tell you to do something, boy, or else you can catch these hands."*

I didn't want any problems and was still in fear even as a grown man, so I pointed to the back door. "Take her to the back and work on her. She doesn't need to be on camera with all of this."

The nurse nodded, removing the last swipe of sweat from her moistened, wrinkled face. I grabbed Mother's elbow as the nurse grabbed the other. We both struggled with lifting her up out of the chair. Mother's eyes became bloodshot red. Either she was losing consciousness, or her blood pressure was sky high. Whatever it was, her body stiffened. Our four hands didn't create enough manpower to lift her up. I was trying hard not to sweat in my new designer suit, but attempting to lift over three hundred pounds of a voluptuous woman was a P90X workout. She jolted, plopping back down into the chair with saliva leaking down her chin. It was too much of a struggle for even her as she exhaled and gripped her chest once again.

Mother lifted her head up, looking back at the cameraman with an *I forbid you* glare. "Remember what I said. Don't nobody call 911. I'm fine. Just a little winded."

Mother Gaines sat next to her, leaning over with a whisper. She held up three fingers, pushing them directly in front of her face.

"Can you see me, Shirley? Look at me. How many fingers am I holding up?" Her big brown eyes magnified three times their size. She looked like she was fully engaged in a science experiment as she gaped at Mother and then back at her fingers again. Her cracked acrylic nails tapped Mother's forearm gently. She looked scared to touch her. Her stretched eyes ogled down as she continued her full inspection with her eyebrows caved in. Mother Gaines wasn't dissecting a fetal pig, and this wasn't an anatomy class, but she treated it as such.

Mother Smithfield blinked back several times and answered, "Gaines? I see you, big googly-eyed gal. Who could miss that raggedy ole gray wig you got on your peanut head? He-he-he."

I covered my mouth, hiding my laughter.

"Feeling better, huh, Mother?" I asked.

If Mother was taking jabs, it was a clear sign that she was back to her abrasive self and the service could carry on.

Some of the members grinned widely in relief, while others looked as if they were praying that she'd closed her eyes for good. She giggled like a child, now finding joy in being catered to in front of a crowd.

I was quite amused, although the look on Mother Gaines' face showed sheer embarrassment. She leaned against her seat, pulling out a compact mirror with an attempt of eliminating the puff in her worn-out wig and fluffed it with her cracked nails.

Mother Smithfield looked back, grinning with her false teeth shifting in her mouth. Her big fake eyelashes had clumped together from the water in the corner of her eyes. Her flared Tina Turner wig turned sideways as she now sat at attention. Her slip was hanging down lower than the length of her flowery handmade dress. She noticed the drop and yanked it up immediately.

The cameras moved to the opposite side of the room. Only the musicians' corner could be viewed. Mother cocked her head back like a Holly Farm chicken this time, standing up on her own with her usual, *I'm black and I'm proud* formation.

No doubt, she was going to remain dignified no matter the occasion. The eyes of the congregation followed her every move as she leaned to the side, holding her silver and black cane for balance. Her gangster lean was fierce with her ham hock legs dipping up and down. Her massive sagging breasts stood at attention and she was now looking ready to march in the next Martin Luther King Jr. parade, rather than in need of medical treatment as we once thought.

When she reached the door of the back room, she smoothed her hands over her thighs and yelled, "It's only a test, children. Stay woke!"

———

I walked back to the podium with my *Wakanda* stride, extricating my temporary nursing duties and shifting back into pastor mode. My practiced hand signals were flashed to the cameraman. Two fingers pointing upward meant to put all cameras back into motion. Four fingers pointing downward meant to flick the red button on the cameras and pause until further notice. A balled fist meant to shut it down quickly all at once. I gave the green light with my two fingers high up in the air. It was back to the regularly scheduled program, with no more dead camera time to spare for the sake of our social media audience.

God's people continued to sit without audible responses. If

I didn't know any better, I would think they could see right through me. My pain, my mistakes, my guilt, my sins.

An eerie feeling came over my body, giving me chills as I heard the words, *"Do the right thing, Henry,"* in my head. For the first time in all my years of preaching, I contemplated giving a church confession. I was adamant about clearing my lying slate at this stage of my life. Right when I got the nerve to come clean, I heard a voice from behind.

"Passuh? The cameras are still rolling. Say something. Why you standing there in a daze? Snap out of it!" Elder Snipes stumbled over to the microphone and put it back in my hand. She then walked back to her seat, pushing her satin striped hat down and pursing her lips with irritation.

I cleared my throat, holding my hands over my ears and praying my way back to reality. *Get it together, Henry! You are a child of God. You are fearfully and wonderfully made. Only God is your judge.*

A new found energy took over as I moved my head from side to side, like a boxer ready to enter the ring for the main event. I investigated the cameras with a fake smile. "It's now time for the Pastoral Prayer, church. Please come on up to the altar and hold your brother or sister's hand."

No one moved.

I doubled back with surprise and gawked into the audience,

motioning my hands for everyone to come forward.

No one moved.

"Well, come on up, church."

Why aren't they following directions? Have they lost their ever-loving minds?

"Lord, have mercy," Mother Gaines scoffed, turning around and looking back at the crowd.

I'm still the lead pastor and overseer of this here church. They better recognize. Years ago, they would've rushed to the altar before I could finish my sentence. Now, they're ignoring me like I'm nothing, a nobody, a has-been. Is this their way of giving a silent protest? What, I can't pray for them anymore? Has it really come to this?

I put my fist up quickly and the cameras blinked off. My tongue felt like a block of ice. For once, I was lost for words. I was a human train wreck standing before them and I'm sure they knew all about it. Yet, I remained unblemished as they continued to sift through my visible skeletons with curious expressions.

I performed an impromptu benediction. Their faces told the story…it was time to go.

I shouted into the crowd, "Let us all stand. Please raise your hands unto the Lord to be dismissed."

Personal items were shuffled while gathering their belongings.

"Amen?"

"Amen," they fired back with their hands lifted high.

"Amen?"

"Amen!" they shouted.

"And, amen again. Be blessed and know that God loves you. You are now dismissed."

PASTOR JONES
CHAPTER 3

ψ I loosened my cufflinks and waved at the last member leaving out the side door of the community center. I took a deep breath, plopping down onto the nearest seat, and scrubbing my arms while allowing my feelings to finally show.

I cried uncontrollably—something I'd never done before. I was weary and tired. I had nowhere to run and nowhere to hide.

"My Lord. Pastor, get yourself together. You're looking like Missy right about now with your eyelids sagging." Deacon Freemon sat beside me, patting my back.

I yelled in agony, mumbling through my fingers. "Father God. Give me strength, Lord."

"It's okay, Pastor. Why are you letting church folks get to you like this? You did your thing up there. They're just used to Missy's preaching style now, that's all," he insisted.

My hands collided with my cheeks. "Why are they treating me like this, Deacon?"

He patted my back like a baby laying on his chest waiting to be burped from an oversized helping of Similac. "God will restore all things new for you in due time, Pastor."

I hunched over. "I just want all of this to go away. That's all."

Deacon Freemon paused, flushed with what looked like a new skin tone as he became pale in the light. "What are we talking about here?"

"So many lies and secrets. I can't keep track anymore." With precarious eyes, he looked at me and said, "Hmm. Tell me which secret and lie you're talking about this time?" He rubbed his hands together as if it was chilly inside the building and took a deep breath. "So, is it true?"

I shook my head back and forth, looking around the room to make sure we were truly alone. Sorrow closed up my throat.

"What, about stealing the money from the church?" He needed to be specific, with all the stuff I had tucked away from church folks.

His eyes stretched with surprise. "No, about Michelle Hanks."

I doubled back, moving to the edge of my seat without responding.

"Are you that baby's pappy, Pastor Jones?" He put his hand on his chin, waiting for an answer and looking like the talk show host Maury Povich with the results envelope in his hand.

It was as if an imaginary stealth bomb came crashing down

from the rooftop and hit me in the middle of my head while I tried to spit it all out. I inhaled and belched words out slowly.

"Heck no, man! Did you really just ask me that?"

His eyebrows rose higher than before.

"That's just straight ungodly, Deacon. Now, I may be wrong about some things, but I ain't that hard up to sleep with Missy's friends." I stood up, feeling insulted and then quickly sat back down again.

He scratched his head, looking confused. "No? Well, who's the father then?"

"Nunna your business, Deacon." I waved my hand, dismissing his comment.

"So, you know who the baby's daddy is, right?"

I wiggled around in my seat, feeling uncomfortable talking about it. "Listen, I consider that gal as one of my children. I've been knowing her since she started preschool. It ain't nobody's business."

"But…"

"But nothing. That's the problem with church folks now. They want to know every cotton pickin' thing about everybody else when their own house is dirty and out of order."

Deacon gave an inquisitive look, agreeing with a nod.

"I don't play when it comes to my children. You know that girl is like a daughter to me."

I slumped my shoulders in relief. "Well, now they got ahold of that rumor and that's why they were acting like that today, huh?"

"Yep."

"I should have known borrowing a little cash wouldn't make them turn on me like that."

"*Oh, now it's borrowing?*" Deacon wailed with laughter. He knew the full story about the money I took from the church. "Don't kid yourself," he grunted. "Anyway. Something always goes wrong with the Joneses."

I shrugged my shoulders. "Yep."

He shook his head. "Always something. Your own brothers don't attend this church for the same reason your members gave you the stink eye today…the drama."

I shook my head. "Ebenezer Light House can have them two. They've been jealous of me since Mama died."

"I'm sure God isn't pleased with any of it." He shook his head.

I made eye contact, not in favor of his smart remark. "God ain't pleased with you running around with all these women in the church either, but you don't hear me talking about it."

Bitterness filled his lips and his eyes prickled with shame. He scratched his head, bending over with his eyes bugged out. I'm sure he was thinking about the car accident that killed his wife, due to his transgressions.

He gulped hard, changing the subject quickly. "All you can do is leave it in God's hands."

He smirked as his eyes seemed to tell all his thoughts.

I smirked back. "Yep, I will get it right one day."

He switched back to the topic at hand with an indulgent tone. "So, with Michelle being in jail, where's the baby?"

"At my house with First Lady."

He tugged his shirt collar with surprise. "Huh?"

"You heard right, Negro. Your daughter, Natalia, changed her mind about taking him in, remember? Who else was going to keep him?"

His eyes stretched. "Her family maybe?"

I shook my head back and forth. "They don't want that boy. Long story."

He sat with an inquisitive look, waiting to hear all about it.

"Anyway, I'm going to confess about the money thing and then clear my name with the rest when I get a chance."

Deacon's eyes rolled in the back of his head with his hand waving back and forth. "Uh-uh. Don't do it, *bruh*. Clearing your name is cool but giving confessions about stealing to a congregation full of black folks is plumb suicide. You're asking for trouble."

"How?"

"Trust me on this one."

I rubbed my beard hairs from side to side in deep thought.

He held up his index finger with surety. "And you will lose members too."

We sat silently sharing a long stare. Minutes later, we both gave each other the look, signaling it was time to go home. We walked out the side door without mumbling a word. I jumped into my Cadillac, wondering, *how can I make all of this right?*

I wasn't worried about what the church thought of me, but I was very worried about what they thought of Michelle. She'd been through enough. Child molestation, drugs, a baby, murder, and now jail time…she just couldn't catch a break. A young intelligent girl that had more secrets then I did. One thing was for sure, no one could ever find out who fathered her baby…no one.

MISSY

CHAPTER 4

Beanie jumped from the bed, leaping onto the hardwood floor, and making loud thumping sounds. He ran into the living room, leaving his Jamaican-flag-colored flip flops behind. He was full of rage as if someone was chasing him. I was awakened from all the commotion and wiped my blurry eyes for understanding.

I threw on my pink robe, jumped out of bed, and ran behind him. We squared up in the middle of the vibrant colored living room, stopping in front of my Dracaena Silk artificial plant that shifted towards the left side of the sofa. Our feet aligned across from one another at the same time. My cat, Twinkles, stood at attention, looking up at both of us.

My voice trembled. "What's wrong?"

He responded, out of breath, and holding his neck in agony. "So, you gonna play me like you don't know what just happened, Missy?" His eyes were glossy, and scratches were across his dark mocha skin.

"Can you please tell me what's going on, so we can go back to bed?" My hands felt slick as I rubbed them together, bracing myself.

He talked fast with a growl. His Jamaican slang words and broken English combined created an entirely new language.

"Me lady! Are you kidding me? Ya' choked me in your sleep." His muscular chest rose up in front of me with exaggerated breaths.

"How was I supposed to know what I was doing to you? All I can do is say I'm so sorry." I intentionally batted my eyes, trying to gain sympathy. I could tell by the firm tone in his voice that the eye batting wasn't going to fly this time.

I must've been fighting my dead abusive boyfriend, Tommy, in my dreams. The man's been dead for almost a year but he's still haunting me.

"Yeah, you're sorry alright. A sorry American wo…" he paused, realizing he was about to cross the line with his alpha male attitude. "Stop pretending that everything is okay and get some help."

I frantically huffed loudly. "I'm not pretending. Jesus is my help."

He marched around the sofa, swishing his arms back and forth. "You and your prideful daddy act like nothing ever goes wrong with a Jones. If you ask me, y'all are some jacked up church folks."

ı Excuse me?

His foot stomped, making a loud crash against the tarnished wood.

I tried to keep calm. "What do you expect me to do, Beanie?"

A guttural tone lashed out of his mouth. "Get back on your meds ASAP; that's what I expect."

I slammed my arms down, restraining my hands to my side. I didn't want to haphazardly choke him out. Instead, I stood there amazed at his level of anger towards me.

Now, this is new.

"I don't need a shrink guiding my footsteps anymore. God's got this."

"Well, guess what, Little Miss Pastor?" His eyes flickered like flames from a candle. "God created doctors, medication, psychotherapy, and counselors for people just like you. So, you better do something before you become Durham's next single black female."

I could feel my eyes stretching in his direction. I dashed around the sofa, inching closer with balled up fists. "What did you just say to me?"

He bunched his hands together, holding them in the middle of his chest. "You heard me, woman!" His index finger shook recklessly in my direction. "As the saying goes, you take the first

35

step and allow God to take two. Be wise, me lady, 'cause this is nuts." His finger was shaking faster and now even closer to my face.

That finger action needs to cease.

The infamous anxiety bug crept in between us as my feet started tapping. "I don't know what to say, Beanie."

"Heck, I know what to say. You need to get some help before you kill me!" He rubbed his fingertips around his neck again, brushing over his wounds. He adjusted the elastic from his Black Panther briefs. His eyelids drooped. I could tell that I had drained him emotionally and now here I was hurting him physically too. Not my intent at all. Unfortunately, he was taking the brunt of something that had nothing to do with him.

I moved in closer to examine his neck, grabbing a piece of tissue from the coffee table's Kleenex stash. The bruises were deep and welled up within his skin. Drops of blood circulated around each scar as I tried to blot the blood away as quickly as it seeped out.

"It doesn't look so bad," I whispered.

He held his fingertips to his lips, talking through them and looking deeply into my eyes. "I can't keep living like this."

"I know. I'm so sorry."

His brows drew together with disdain. "I didn't sign up for all of this *crap*."

I see he's not going to let this go now, is he?

╹I removed the tissue and dropped my hand away. I stepped back, making a steeple with my fingers. The look in his eyes signified the love meter had plummeted. The anger suffused his features. He threw a stone-cold glance, looking me up and down. His vibrant and jolly expression that used to be shown each time he gazed in my direction was now erased. I put my head down in shame, tapping my foot even harder. I didn't have answers, nor did I have a cure. This thing called anxiety had heightened and was driving me to an unknown and unfamiliar place. My feelings were jumbled, and I was giving out of steam. Trying to maintain a relationship while getting myself together was becoming way too much for me.

MISSY

CHAPTER 5

I slept on the futon in the guest room last night and rose with a new attitude. I rushed to the kitchen to fix a full breakfast with pancakes, eggs, and sausages on my mini-griddle countertop contraption.

After thirty minutes of kitchen mastery, I made some fresh Starbucks brand coffee with the automated Farberware I ordered from the Home Shopping Network a few weeks ago. Within seconds, the coffee pot beeped as I reached for the mugs placed beside it and prepared some steaming hot mocha for the two of us.

Minutes later, Beanie joined me at the kitchen table. I was in a daze, staring into his pretty brown eyes as he sat across from me with a wrinkled forehead. I sipped on my mocha latte, hoping he would forgive me somehow, with a slight gesture of head nodding or a sheepish smile. But, that wasn't going to happen as his thick accent spouted out angry words, helping me to regain my focus.

"So, are you going to get some help or what, me lady? 'Cause if not, I'm taking my black behind back to the island." He picked up his fork, stuffing a piece of egg white in his mouth.

"Really? Is this how you wake up these days?"

"Yep," he responded, mashing pancake into his mouth, complementing the egg white.

"Can't we start the morning off talking about something else?"

He frowned, answering abruptly and throwing his fork in his plate, "No, we can't."

The imaginary safety pin he poked in my heart pricked me deeply. I responded with a remorseful tone, sitting up tall in my seat. "Why do you say stuff like this? When you love someone, you work with them."

"Well, I'm still here working with you, so it's up to YOU to make it right. I swear, woman...." He stopped in mid-sentence, pushing his coffee mug into his lips. He slurped with hate streaking across the table.

I sucked in air and answered, "I hear you, Beanie Anderson. Whatever you say."

"Is that all you have to say? I wanted to hear...hey, babe, I think that's a good idea. Or, hey babe, I will call a doctor sometime today."

I gave him the thumbs up and answered. "Yep. What you said." I slammed my half-filled cup of coffee on the table and folded my arms. I was no longer interested in my bountiful breakfast. My appetite fled.

I stared down at my engagement ring and then back at him. "So, I guess this means nothing, huh?"

He pulled his chair beside me, stroking my hair and holding my face while kissing me on my forehead. His facial expression changed completely once he took notice of the shining ring that he paid thousands of dollars for. "I want the best for you, Missy. I really do. But if you won't get some help…I gotta do something different. I won't allow you to make me lose my mind because you won't get help for yours."

"What do you mean?"

Is he calling me crazy on the low? Or does "doing something different" mean another woman?

"Take it how you want to take it, me lady. You're not the only one in this room that can turn heads."

My vision blurred while guilt flooded over my face. It was too early in the morning for this type of disappointment. I took his hand and began to pray. "Dear Lord…"

He snatched it back and said, "God puts doctors in place for a reason, Missy. Don't sugarcoat this issue with your Pentecostal prayers. You better be making some phone calls this morning, or else."

Hold me, Jesus. Just hold me. I feel a jab connecting to his face real soon.

"Or else what?" I blurted.

He walked back into the bedroom, swinging his arms from side to side and ignoring the question. I followed right behind him. Breakfast was officially *over.*

He laid down on the bed, pulling the comforter back and fluffing his goose pillow. No further eye contact was made as he turned his head and rolled over without saying another word.

"Isn't it time for you to go to work?"

"I've decided to take the day off. Dealing with you this morning just made me *sick.*" He slapped his head with his hand.

I stood on my side of the bed, burning with humiliation. I wanted to make things right and I definitely wanted him to stay with me. He used to be really good to me up until now. I couldn't deny that. But, this was a side of him that I hadn't seen before.

\My mouth turned dry as his words chilled my soul. I was too weak to cry and too dumbfounded to think straight. I began to get down on my knees at the foot of the bed but this time I prayed *alone.*

ᐟThe telephone rang loudly while ending my prayer. I picked it up carefully and walked into the living room.

A robotic voice came across the line. "You have a call from the North Carolina Correctional Institution for Women. Do you accept the charges?"

Is this Michelle calling from prison trying to apologize for all of her years of betrayal?

"Yes, I accept," I answered, disgruntled.

A crackling voice spoke rapidly, "Missy, is that you?"

I contemplated if I should hang up or stay on the line. I knew that voice from anywhere.

"Olivia?"

"Yes, dear its *Olivia*. Is that you Missy?"

"Yes, Olivia, it's me. Why are you calling me?"

She paused. "I got to thinking."

"Yeah, I bet that hurt," I said with sarcasm.

"Seriously, Missy. Life isn't promised, and I realized I was hurting the wrong person. You have nothing to do with your father's broken promises and I owe you an apology."

"You don't say?" I looked back down the hallway to ensure that Beanie wasn't listening in on my conversation. He told me long ago not to trust Olivia no matter what, and here I was talking to her as if nothing happened.

"I want to get to know you better, my child. Can you come

and visit me this week?"

Huh? You burn the church down and now you want to talk? Where is all of this coming from?

I hesitated. "I really don't see a need for us to meet. You've done enough damage."

"Don't be afraid of me, my love. Prison time has been good for me. I'm not the woman you used to know."

Yeah, right. The devil is a liar.

"Please forgive me for my childish behavior in the past. I wish I could go back in time and fix all my mistakes. I can't replace the church, but I can at least replace our lost relationship. Can we start over, my love?"

Ms. Poetic Justice is talking good right about now.

I didn't say a word.

"I feel positive vibes about us getting together. I look forward to seeing your beautiful brown eyes real soon. Okay?"

"Maybe." I scoffed.

I slammed the phone down, looking away in disbelief. While I wanted to prove to Beanie that I could change, Olivia wanted to prove to me the same.

After all she's done to destroy the Jones family, now she wants to suddenly kiss and make up? She sounds sincere. But is she?

NATALIA

CHAPTER 6

My heart fluttered with joy, watching the snow fall in chunks from the living room window. The Forest Hills area was so pretty this time of the year. I was just getting adjusted as a new homeowner planning for the holidays. New black art paintings leaned up against the walls in the hallway and dining area. Frank was planning to put them all up before the weekend. I'm sure they would accentuate the caramel colored walls that took us weeks to complete. It was a beautiful four-bedroom home with lavishing upgrades.

The nostalgia of Christmas with the love of my life made me tingle all over. I never thought I would find someone like Frank Thomas. He was loving, caring, and some kind of wonderful. Every second we shared together was a supernatural experience. God had created this man just for me.

Mr. Wonderful sat in the living room with his toned dark legs crossed and shining oiled lips that he puckered up, waiting for a kiss. I reached over, plopping a wet one that covered his entire mouth. His lips tasted like cinnamon from the piece of gum he chewed. His saliva sloshed with mine, latching tongue to tongue.

I'd outgrown male bashing once I met him. But then again, I'd outgrown a lot of things. Between gaining a relationship with God and meeting my soulmate, my life was complete. Those long conversations with my advocacy group, *Black Girls Reign,* about the 21st century men used to be so negative back in the day. Now I can go to the next meeting, snapping my fingers in the air, and saying, *"Yes, ladies, there are a few good men left in Durham. Halleluyer."*

Things were going so well between us that Frank decided to stay with me from time to time, making a bed out of my plush red leather sofa. He was a gentleman to the fullest and honored my wishes of waiting for intimacy until marriage.

I kissed him again before getting up and walking into the kitchen, ready to prepare dinner. I reached into the refrigerator, staring at the skimpy meal choices. I bought a large pack of turkey meat from Food Lion a few days ago and it would go perfect with my scalloped potatoes I cooked the night before.

Meatloaf, maybe?

I asked with an alluring tone while reaching down to get the pack of meat out of the fridge, "What do you want for dinner, sweetness?"

"Whatever you fix. I'm not hungry just yet, babe. I'm meeting the fellas downtown."

"Oh, really?" My head popped up.

"Yeah, I want to watch the Panthers whoop up on Green Bay tonight." He turned his neck toward the kitchen and continued talking, "Did you know that the new sports bar next to the ball park has a huge movie projector in the center of the building? It's one of the largest screens in the area."

Not at all interested in the new restaurant's amenities, I answered back, "Yeah, I heard."

I sucked my teeth, walking over to the counter and slamming the raw meat down. The onion bits bottle turned over and caught his attention. He turned completely around, looking back with wonderment over his face.

I left the meat on the counter in disgust and walked to the sink to wash my hands.

So much for meatloaf.

I went back into the living room, gyrating my hips back and forth. My lips poked out intentionally as I sunk my bottom into the sofa right beside him. He leaned over, stretching his arms with a look of concern.

"Nat, listen. I just want to enjoy a Monday night football game with the fellas, that's all." He winked, reaching for an embrace. "Can you handle that?"

I simpered at his masculinity as he swayed his long legs back and forth. He could always give me a few prickling sensations of excitement even when I wanted to be mad at him. I looked him deep into his eyes and said, "Enjoy yourself, honey."

His eyebrows caved in as he flashed an inverted smile. "Well, I'm glad to hear you say that. Most women would have a problem with me hanging out, after being on lockdown in a snowstorm over the weekend with their woman."

I laughed because back in the day, the boisterous, no-holds-barred Natalia would have been that female to do just that. I remained calm, squeezing out the words I didn't mean, "You're good with me, baby. See you when you get back."

His shoulders dropped, releasing the tension. He grabbed me closer to his slender chest and whispered in my ear, "I promise you, girl, I will come back at a decent time. Cool?"

I reached over, holding his face in the palm of my hands and responding with a long romantic kiss. "I will be right here when you get back, baby."

His eyes gave subliminal messages of *I want you, girl* as my legs buckled. I wanted to keep my new-found salvation, but he looked doggone good today. My flesh had me sweating all down my shirt.

He doubled back, still eye to eye, and said, "You know one

day you're going to be my wife, right? And when that wonderful day happens, I'm going to make love to you every chance I get."

Bruh, stop talking like that right now.

I pinched the bridge of my nose, pushing up my gold-rimmed glasses. He was good at making my spectacles steam. At that moment, he was looking like a big bowl of chocolate ice cream that I wanted to scoop up and gulp down quickly. Being around him without getting physical was difficult. But, I made a promise to God and he respected that.

"No, actually, I didn't know that," I answered.

"You just wait and see, girl. You will be the most beautiful bride in all of Durham. I'm going to make sure of that."

His lips locked onto my forehead as he stood up, lean and tall. "I'll be back in a few."

He swung around to pick up his jacket like a male model, replanted his feet, and walked towards the door, gleaming. He smirked back at me as if he was the luckiest man in the world when he reached the doorway and said, "Have that old-fashioned meatloaf ready for me when I get back, sweet lips."

It was 11:30 pm. I paced the hardwood floor, wondering, *what should I say when he comes in smelling like another woman?* Paranoia set in after watching a full *Scandal* marathon. Missy once preached that if we didn't want bad thoughts implanted in our heads, stop watching certain sitcoms. But who could give up on *Scandal?* The more the character Olivia Pope kissed the president, the more antsy I got about my man being unfaithful.

Lord, why do I put myself through this?

I changed the channel as the phone rang. I shoved my earpiece in and said, "Hello?"

"Hey, Nat," Missy's soft voice filled my Bluetooth.

"What's up, chick?"

"What are you and Frank up to on this cold and snowy night?"

I paused. "I'm just sitting here twiddling my fingers waiting for Frank to come home. He went out with some friends."

"Oh." She paused.

"What are you up to?"

"I was calling to see if Beanie was with him. I've been calling his cell phone for hours and haven't gotten a call back yet."

I blew my breath. "Let the man have some time away, Missy. Jesus."

"Yeah, I try to give him space but I'm so afraid that one of these days, he won't come back."

"Well, with all of your theatrics over Tommy, I'd be ready to leave your behind too. Do you blame him? Plus, you're a pastor with a live-in boyfriend. Now how does that look to church folks? Maybe Beanie's acting up because God's bringing down the wrath." I chuckled.

She sighed. "Whatever."

"Whatever?" I put my hand on my hips as if she could see me through the phone.

"I'm not having sex with him; we just happened to share the same bed at night."

"That needs to change also, don't you think?"

She paused again. "It doesn't matter. He wouldn't touch me right about now even if I wanted him to. I've been sleeping on the futon for the last week."

"Glooorrrryyyy. Yes, hontey, yes." I snapped my fingers with agreement.

"You're so silly."

"That's so wonderful. It's sad it took him to put an end to your fornication reign and not 'The Pastor' herself. But, whatever works. So, tell me this then; have you stopped crying over Tommy, the dead man, yet?"

Her voice became muffled. "Why do you always make me out to be the bad person? I can't make mistakes like most humans?"

"Sure, you can, but you know better. Folks that know better should do better. You can't preach deliverance and salvation, when you're doing everything that you're telling the people of

God not to do."

"I know. I'm chugging along with all of it. I realize my faults, Nat, and I'm correcting them day by day. I've even been contemplating stepping down to take some time off and reflect on my life. Maybe take a vacation or something. Another girl's trip, maybe?"

"Glory to his nammmmmeeeee. Now you are getting it, girlfriend." I snapped my fingers again. "But, not interested in the girl trip though."

"Some friend you are. Anyway, I'm glad you find yourself so amusing. If you see Beanie…"

Before she could complete her sentence, I heard a key turn in the door.

Frank? He's home before midnight? Gosh, I love this man.

"I'm sorry to cut you off, Missy, but I've got to go now. I'll ask Frank if he's heard anything from Beanie. I'll chat tomorrow."

I dropped the call instantly, not concerned about her reply. I rushed to the door and hugged Frank tightly as soon as he took two steps onto the foot area rug. The welcome home kiss signaled I was ready to cuddle for the next six to eight hours.

"Well, someone is glad to see me."

"Yes, I'm very glad to see you, handsome."

He leaned over me, holding my hips tightly. "Good,

because I thought about you the entire time. I don't know what it is, Nat, but I finally feel complete. All the money I make, all the traveling that I do, doesn't compare to being here holding you. I haven't had these kinds of feeling in years. We've only been together for six months and I'm ready to jump the broom with you, baby girl." He looked me up and down. "With your fine self."

I blushed.

"You better be ready to pull out that passport, baby girl. As soon as this weather lets up, we are going to travel the world together."

Those flattering words took me to another place in my mind. I could see us vacationing from country to country on my flight attendant discount. Not that we needed it because his technology company was raking in the dough. But, I had to contribute in some kind of way. I would be laying across a hammock with my favorite sushi roll covered with tiny pieces of ginger. Meanwhile, he would be rubbing my size-eight feet down with cocoa butter and putting a champagne glass up to my mouth. Beyoncé and Jay Z's song, "'03 Bonnie & Clyde" would be playing in the background as my hips swayed against his chest in a three-colored, two-piece bathing suit.

"Earth to Nat?"

I zoomed back in, gazing at his deep smile. Meanwhile,

inside my body, my ovaries were about to burst. Warmth filled my chest and without hesitation, I had to reveal how I felt for him. Normally, I would hold onto the words *I love you* and allow the man to say it first, but I couldn't with him; he was different.

I blew my breath and wailed, "I'm in love with you, Frank Thompson." I exhaled deeply. "There, I said it."

He bent down, giving me a hug. "Whoa. Natalia Freemon just revealed her feelings? Where is WRAL when you need them?"

I chuckled.

"Now that is an amazing accomplishment. Way to go, sweet lips."

He reached down and kissed me with passion and fire oozing out. I was mesmerized. I couldn't believe I finally used the three heartfelt words that I refused to use with anyone else. But by now, he deserved to hear it. I looked him up and down, licking my lips.

He makes me want to sin now and repent later.

I tugged on his arm, pulling him towards the bedroom. After revealing my heart, I was ready to give him all of me.

He pulled back. "Now wait a minute, we promised each other that we wouldn't go near the bedroom when we're feeling randy like this."

"Yeah, and..." I said with a hot and bothered panting tone.

"We'll lay on the sofa until we get tired. Going to the bedroom right about now won't keep our promise."

I whispered softly, trying to play innocent, "You think so?" *But I just poured out my feelings, man!*

He coughed. "I know so. I may be a saved man, but I'm not a virgin one. You're looking too good right now and I won't be able to control my hands. And the fact that you're finally expressing yourself too…now I'm turned all the way on."

I had the urge to suck on his face. I mushed my mouth into his lips. As his thick chopper bumped against mine, I melted like a pack of sea salt butter in a deep iron skillet. My hormones were on ten.

"Okay, the sofa is fine," I hissed in disappointment.

"Good choice," he said with seductive eyes and a deep frown.

It was a smoking hot lustful moment that wasn't conducive for either of us. I had to change the subject fast, quick, and in a hurry. I cleared my throat, trying to talk normal as we waltzed to the seating area. "By the way, was Beanie with you tonight?"

He moved his head back, looking down at me. "Yeah, he stopped through to watch some of the game. Why you ask?"

"Missy was worried, that's all."

He rolled his eyes. He didn't like to engage in any conversation pertaining to Missy Jones. He showed disdain for her often. He viewed her as the selfish, fornicating brat and Beanie should've taken off a long time ago. Double dating was out of the question and he especially didn't attend Mt. Zion, knowing that Missy was preaching fire and brimstone with hidden issues. He referred to Mt. Zion as the blind leading the blind. Because of the apparent friction between them, we decided early on in our relationship to attend his church, Ebenezer Lighthouse, until we figured it all out.

I leaned into his chest, pinning him with my eyes and speaking softly, "I thank God for you."

He squeezed me tightly, leaning his head on my shoulder.

He responded, "I thank God for you too. Oh, and most of all, I love you too, Natalia Freemon."

Dear God, please tuck my hormones away until my wedding day.

MICHELLE

CHAPTER 7

The bright lights in the prison visitation room had Micah squinting up at me. I held him close, squeezing his little fingers tightly. He reached for my hair strands, pulling them down closer to his tiny face. I wish I could hold him in my arms for eternity. I smiled back at his loud cooing, rocking him back and forth. He smelled like a cross between cocoa butter and baby-scented shampoo. He was my miracle baby and destined for greatness.

His tight grip made my eyes fill up with water. When I looked at him, I was reassured that living this dreadful life of mine was worth living. I made several attempts to end my life while in prison. From slitting my wrists, to taking an excessive number of pills, getting high off unknown substances; you name it, I did it. But, for some reason, God kept me here on this earth time and time again. So, it's obvious, I'm spared for this little man of mine. His big bright eyes flashing back at me somehow made me feel important.

"So, how you been doing, gal?" Pastor Jones asked.

"As expected, I guess, in this place."

"Are the other girls being nice to you in here?" First Lady Jones asked with a smug expression, looking down on the raw cuts on my wrist.

"I guess you can say that." I looked back at Micah, ignoring her beaming eyes.

"Have you seen Olivia in here yet?" Pastor Jones said with candor.

"Yeah, unfortunately, I've seen her more than I would like to. Don't know what's up with her, but she's supposed to be getting released soon."

"Released? What do you mean?"

"I'm just repeating what I heard. I have no idea, Pastor."

He stomped his foot in rage, making thudding noises. "I don't understand this justice system. I guess it's okay to burn down a historical church and not do the time for the crime?" First Lady shrugged her shoulders as they exchanged looks.

Visiting every Sunday after church became routine. Pastor said it was important that I make a solid connection with Micah. His wife, who didn't have an ounce of Jesus in her, always seemed to look down on me as if I was an alien child from an unknown planet. She had Pastor wrapped around her finger and it was hard to watch such a powerful man turn into a little boy over a sin-filled woman. She had long flowing hair and was younger and shorter than his first wife. She resembled Missy and Olivia somewhat, with the fair skin and big pretty eyes. The difference was she wasn't poised or girly-like. She walked like a floozy parading out of a night club, because she had big clunky feet and wide hips that didn't match her small frame. Her large hips flapped off her body and always seemed to poke out of her shimmery designer pantsuits. Skirts were not invented for a funny-shaped woman like her.

It was evident that I didn't care for her and the feelings were mutual. She only tagged along every Sunday to keep an eye on Micah. He grew on her and I could tell she was getting attached to him too. Without having the ability to have children, it was expected. However, new found motherhood didn't take away her bad attitude.

"You eating in here? You are looking mighty skinny, gal," Pastor asked, looking me up and down with a leery look.

"Not always. But, I try to eat as much as I can. Don't have an appetite these days."

"I see. Whelp, it's almost time for us to leave, gal. Let me run to the little boy's room before we push that Cadillac down Highway 40. Be right back, ladies."

He walked slowly out of the room with his trench coat brushing against his chins. First Lady Jones snapped her neck around once the coast was clear.

"Listen, young lady. I don't mind these visits, but when you get out of here, you won't be getting Micah back," she grunted.

I rocked Micah even harder. "What?"

"Henry and I love Micah and he brings life back into our home. I'm sure with a little bit of Henry's money, you will be convinced to walk away from motherhood, just like Olivia did back in the day for Missy."

I couldn't believe her cold words. I felt my nose flaring up. "Let me tell you something, First Lady Jones, this boy is my life…" I felt like cursing in Spanish, French, and Bahamian after that comment.

"I bet you don't even know where the other half is, do you?"

My skin boiled. I aligned my body to look at her eye to eye. "Looka here, you do realize I killed someone to get in here, right?"

She cleared her throat with a big gulp, putting her hands over her mouth. "And? What does that mean?" She gathered up her satin coat, threw it across her shoulders, and said, "You don't scare me."

I loomed in. "Well, you should be scared, because I'm very good with knives. Especially long ones."

She didn't mutter a sound after that. Her face was flushed,

and her hands were trembling.

Seconds later, Pastor Jones slid back into his seat. "What y'all over here talking about?"

I gave First Lady the evil eye and responded, "Oh, nothing much. Just going over all of Micah's new milestones."

"Yeah, that boy moves around like he's been here before. I got some of it on video. You want to see it?"

First Lady interjected, pulling Micah out of my arms. "Give me the baby. It's time to go, Henry."

I felt sad and withdrawn enduring another goodbye.

I waved, unbothered by her ignorance. "Bye-bye, beautiful baby. Mommy will be home to get you real soon."

She used her free hand, swiping the remnants of red lipstick across her lips.

"I suppose I will show you the videos next Sunday, gal. If it's the Lord's will. You take care of yourself, chile." Pastor Jones stood up, brushing himself off.

First Lady turned around, heading towards the door and not looking back. Pastor Jones gave me a bear hug and said, "Alright, Michelle, be good now and pray without ceasing, ya hear?"

Tears began to roll rapidly down my cheek. I didn't want my baby to leave me.

"It's going to be okay, daughter. God is handling this.

You'll be out of here before you know it."

A mask of moisture filled my eyelids. "Okay." I grabbed him tightly.

He returned the hug and then pulled back, quickly zipping up his jacket. He covered his head with his stylish fedora that matched his coat. He gave a closing remark just like he would do in church before making his final exit. "Heal, gal. All you can do is heal. The faster you gain a complete relationship with God, the faster the healing process will begin."

I looked up at him like a kid that adored her parent. "Thank you for that, Pastor."

I turned around, wiped my tears, and headed back through the steel doors that led to hell. The recordings of my life could make a *Lifetime* movie one day. Memories started to fly around inside my head. With every image resurfacing, I felt dirty and nasty inside. I remembered the night Micah was conceived like it was yesterday.

The man that implanted the seed in my womb for a second time was none other than my biological father, Andrew Hanks. He came back to town to settle an estate. But his first stop was my house to manipulate, conquer, and devour my soul. I was his prized possession after years of child molestation and it wasn't surprising that one day he would return with an attempt to finish what he once started.

He came to my house one early Sunday morning. I was getting ready for church and I heard the doorbell ring. Mama yelled up the stairs, "Michelle, you have company. I need to go to the store; I'll be back."

I can remember thinking, who would she let in our home and then leave for the store? When the door slammed shut, I peeped down the stairs to see who it was. My father's dingy looking face turned towards the stairway, meeting me eye to eye. I felt like a vulnerable little girl again. A woman who was supposed to be my rock, my support system, my protector…left me alone with this predator?

Andrew Hanks marched up the stairs as his steel-toed boots clanged against the wood. I ran back in my room and locked my door crumbling near the side of the bed. With three attempts of opening the door, he kicked the door in. He rushed over and pulled me by my collar, with my feet dangling in the air.

"Surprise! Daddy's home," he chanted.

I fought hard and broke free from his clutch, running around to the other side of the bedroom. He slid across the bed and reached over, grabbing my shirt and ripping it completely off my backside. We tussled for several minutes like two men fighting in the streets. He eventually grabbed my neck, kicked me down with his hard boots onto the floor, and plopped his heavyweight sagging belly against my body.

"Noooo!" I screamed, scratching and punching him in the head.

My little hands didn't do much damage to his strong and husky build.

He proceeded with ease, forcing my skirt up and draping it over my head. I screamed and cried, pushed and shoved, kicked, bit, and spit, trying desperately to get away from his stronghold. But, nothing worked.

"Look at you, putting up a fight. You missed your daddy, didn't you?"

"Get away from me, you monster. Help. Stop it. You're evil. I hate you!"

We tussled back and forth like we were in a wrestling match.

"I've been trying to get back to Durham for years, just for you, sweet darling. I missed this thang," he mumbled, looking down at my private parts.

He pressed down on my arms, finding a way to tie my hands with the shredded pieces of my shirt that laid before him. I scooted around, trying to kick my way to freedom. He remained on top of me, pulling his belt through his pants loops and tugging them downward, while pinning me to the floor. I could feel my skin rip each time I pulled away as droplets of blood dripped down my face. The dreadful five minutes was worse than anything I had ever experienced. When I was a child, I didn't know what he was doing to me was something terribly wrong. But, as an adult, I had a choice and I wasn't going down without a fight. Right then, I wanted the Lord to snatch me into heaven. Leaving this earth instead of enduring more abuse from this man would have been a blessing.

"Momma, where are you? How could you leave me?" I screamed, hoping that she would be somewhere in the house to save me from this

terrible reunion.

He pulled his pants up with satisfaction, wiping blood off his arms, and whispered. "I bet you'll never forget me, huh, gal? Who's your daddy?"

I spit in his face as he slapped me across mine. He rose up and tipped out of the room like a thief in the night, robbing me of pride, strength, and perseverance.

I couldn't move, I couldn't think, and I hated life. I rocked back and forth right where he left me. Micah Hanks was conceived from his granddaddy's sperm without my consent and no one heard my cry. No one cared. No one came to save me that day, not even God.

MICHELLE

CHAPTER 8

I woke up the next morning, trying to erase the dreadful thoughts of that day out of my memory. It was breakfast for the inmates, but food was the last thing on my mind. I walked up to the guard that stood near my cell, asking, "What you got for me today, Sam?"

He looked around, hovering over, and said, "I got something new for you to try. You want it?"

"Yes." I blinked.

"Have a seat, my friend."

Smuggling drugs inside for prisoners was easy for Sam. He had been working in the prison for over twenty years and he made drug pushing his part-time job.

I sat down in his guard seat next to my cell with my eyes following his hands. He pressed down into his pocket, reaching for a piece of foil. I opened it, gawking down at a big crystal rock that resembled a ball of sugar.

"What's this, Sam? Do I sniff it or eat it?" Curiosity prompted me to move in closer. He took another piece out of his pocket and demonstrated as he pushed the damp crystal up his nose. I followed right behind him.

Within seconds I could no longer feel the chair against my backside. This wasn't an ordinary high. This was heaven.

"You got more?" I sniffed the crumbs back into my nose, embracing the splendor of this new-found substance.

"Slow down, lil' mama. Don't hurt yourself."

I raised my voice, propping my elbows against the chair. "I said, do you have more, Sam?"

He passed another ball of crystal, slapping it into my hands with a pretend handshake.

"See, little mama, I know what you like. This is better than pills, right?"

Indeed.

Each sniff helped me to erase the visions of my father's slimy body against mine. I licked the foil dry as my tongue numbed in motion. I wanted every speck of this new found good stuff. It was food for my soul.

He looked over with a question mark stare. "So, when you gonna pay me, lady?"

I tried zooming back in as my nose twitched from the new sensation. "Next week. Yeah, next week I will pay you."

Pastor Jones put money on my books every Friday. Little did he know it was going straight to the drug smuggling security guard.

"Now that's what I'm talking about, lil' lady. Care for another piece?"

I nodded my head, sniffing another. I hunched over with the inability to control my muscles. I should have been lacing my fingers in prayer and fighting off this thing called addiction. But instead I cuddled it, craved it, and made love to it right where I sat.

Before I could sniff it all up my nose, my head bobbled like a puppet and I fell out of the chair and onto the hard-cemented floor. I was once sleep deprived, but not after sniffing this wonderful sleep-inducing substance. With my eyes closed shut, I hoped to see Jesus during my comatose state.

Lights out. It's nap time.

PART II

ONE DAY AT A TIME SWEET JESUS.

"Refuse to worry about tomorrow, but deal with each challenge that comes your way, one day at a time. Tomorrow will take care of itself."

Matthew 6:34

MISSY

CHAPTER 9

Months Later...

❧ I spent the last several months at the prison, gaining a solid relationship with Olivia. I enjoyed the small miracle God rendered in changing her heart. For some strange reason, after months of getting to really know her, I trusted her.

As for Beanie and me, things were getting worse between us. We split the apartment into two sections, his side and my side. He had all his stuff in boxes packed and ready to go back to Jamaica any day now. But the good thing was, we never had another choking incident after that night, because I gave up my bed completely and allowed him to sleep in peace.

The futon became my nightly oasis and I never looked back. We would go days, sometimes weeks, without speaking to one another. But for some reason, I was determined not to give up on our relationship and I still wore my engagement ring with pride.

Nothing seemed to faze him. He was a stubborn man that wasn't going to give in until I followed his advice of seeking help. From long love letters to leaving sticky notes on the bathroom mirror, he ignored them all. I cooked for him, prayed for him out loud, and bought lavish gifts, but he still wasn't satisfied. I didn't want my lingering disability of anxiety to affect our relationship like it did, but it was tearing us completely apart. Beanie Anderson was more than tired of me and he showed it. He started staying out later and later and sometimes, not even coming home at all. He was done.

I couldn't keep all my focus on my ill-mannered boyfriend. I had so many other things that had my attention, such as baby Micah and the *church*. Shortly after finding out about Micah living in my dad's home, my heart softened for the little guy. It wasn't Micah's fault that he didn't have a home and it was easier to swallow, knowing that Tommy nor Daddy was his father. For the record, that's all I really cared about.

It was a warm and breezy Sunday morning. I was dressed in my purple preaching robe, waiting for a glass of water from one of the ushers. I felt dehydrated. I wasn't taking care of myself like I used to. My hair was pulled back in a bun and I wore flat shoes that made my robe drag behind me. No longer did I care about the days of stiletto heels with my hair flowing down my back. I was mentally exhausted and depressed at my situation.

Caring about being the best dressed or best looking in the church didn't apply to me anymore. My nails hadn't been done in weeks and I was losing weight by the minute.

I stood up and walked to the podium, looking out into the audience at Beanie's fiery eyes. I tried to walk and talk, but I struggled to remain balanced with my flat shoes on. I wasn't used to preaching like this as I wobbled from side to side. I felt like I was on a tight rope instead of a solid wooden floor. Who knew that flat shoes would feel so awkward?

Beanie sat with his arms folded on the second row, looking straight ahead. His island Christian values wasn't going to allow him to miss church, no matter how he felt about me. Each time the church doors swung open, he was right there, sitting in that same exact seat.

Will we ever get through this?

I blinked back into the cameras. "Let the church say amen."

"Amen."

"Let the church say amen again."

"Amen," they roared back.

I didn't have time for small talk. I jumped right into the word. "Now turn your Bibles to the book of Ruth."

"Alright now!" Mother Smithfield shouted. "Come on with it, gal."

I viewed both sides of the congregation and noticed Olivia

Wallace sitting near Elder Snipes.

Olivia?

My mouth snapped shut from surprise.

She came to see me?

I was giddy like a little child, pushing fear down my throat and hoping to make a good impression.

"And the Bible tells us...Naomi lost her husband and her children. But when they died, she had no other living relatives in the city of Moab."

"That's right, gal. Talk about it," Mother Gaines uttered.

I continued. "She felt lost without them. How many of you ever felt like that? *Lost.*" I raised my hand along with the crowd.

"Well?" Daddy roared, sitting behind me.

"She decided to go back to Judea. A place of praise."

"Alright now." Mother Smithfield took off her glasses to wipe them clean and shoved them back on again.

"Now, some called Judea the garden of praise."

"Shole did. Go head, gal," Daddy moaned.

"And Naomi knew it would take her days to get to her destination."

"Uh-huh." Daddy nodded.

I kept going as I watched Olivia push up her sunglasses and tilt her hat down. Daddy was clueless that she was even in the midst.

"When Naomi got to her destination she wanted to change her name from Naomi, which meant pleasantness, to Mara, which meant bitterness. She felt giving herself a name that meant bitterness was more fitting for her current situation."

"Well, alright. I hear you talking now, gal!" Deacon Freemon shouted, pulling on his suspenders.

I inhaled deeply as my confidence rose and my voice became louder and louder. "She was left with two Moabite daughters-in-law and being a widow herself, she just wasn't mentally in a good place. I'm sure at one point she lost hope in God. How many of you sometimes lose hope?"

"Come on with it, sis." Elder Snipes stood up, waving her handkerchief in the air and leaning over, exposing the top of her chest. She held her Bible tightly in her left hand and pulled down her tight skirt with the other.

I blew into the microphone, releasing a big hack. God's anointing was all over me. "But, what she didn't realize was God was going to restore her joy. God had not forgotten her."

Olivia stood up beside Elder Snipes, yelling and pointing, "Preach!"

Daddy stood up, pulling out his handkerchief, and wiping sweat off his head, saying, "Gloooorrrryy. Bring it on home, gal."

I'm about to do just that, Daddy. Don't believe me, just watch.

I roared, "No matter what you've been through. No matter what it looks like. It's never too late to walk into your garden of praise because God has not forgotten you. Amen?"

"Amen," the congregation confirmed with a few Hallelujahs echoing in the background.

Beanie was now paying attention. My voice started shaking once our eyes met. "And guess what, church? You're not your circumstance." I pointed slightly in Olivia's direction as she covered her mouth, suppressing a smile. She knew that line was meant for her.

"You know when my joy will be restored, church?"

"When?" Mother Gaines shouted as if I was speaking only to her. She was my biggest church cheerleader and stood up the entire time.

"When I go back to seeking professional help for my anxiety. I need my joy restored too. Amen?"

I looked back at Daddy, knowing my testimony would pinch a nerve. He had the *Oh no she didn't* look smeared across his face. His eyes were glazed over as if he wanted to snatch the microphone out of my hands and hide it behind his back.

"I'm not ashamed to give my testimony, because I know Jesus. It's time out for all the secrets and caring about the judgment of man. My only judge is God. Amen?" I pointed to the ceiling.

"Amen."

"I make mistakes with my flesh, just like everyone else that has a pulse."

"Testify, gal!" Mother Gaines shouted, gyrating in circular motion.

"Amen."

"You think my anointing stops my struggles? If anything, it makes them worse."

"Well," Elder Snipes responded, popping bubble gum loudly.

The audience stood up, clapping and praising God before I could finish my next sentence. A spirit of acceptance filled the room and there wasn't a dry eye to be seen.

Mother Gaines looked ecstatic about the word and positioned her body as if she was about to run a marathon.

The praises were rising high.

As the teenagers would say in Sunday school, "This service is on fleek."

The next few lines were about to seal the deal and get the Holy Ghost party started. I could feel the fire shut up all within my bones.

"And guess what, church? When you start your new walk into your Garden of Praise, never look back."

I winked at the cameras, giving the cue to fire up the organ.

I looked over at Daryl and shouted, "Hit them keys, brotha. You know what time it is."

The musical section cranked up like a Mustang car engine. Mother Gaines took off running around the building. The other mothers on the front row danced in a circle, shouting in unison, "Thank ya, Father God."

The crowd went bonkers.

I swayed back and forth to the music while shouting over it, "If you need prayer right where you sit or stand, pray with us now. Grab your sister's or brother's hand."

The congregation bum-rushed to the front, instead of staying near their seats. Seconds later, the cameraman lost control. The spirit hit him dead in the back and he ran up and down the aisle, shouting, "Thank You, Jesus!"

Deacon Freemon rushed over, fumbling with the cameras. He made a failed attempt to keep them rolling. The big screens flashed in and out as the Holy Spirit made an imaginary wave across the congregation.

Beanie came over and stood right in front of me. His lips touched my earlobe. He whispered, "Well done, baby. Your breakthrough has arrived. Thank you for taking one step..."

I finished his sentence, "And allowing God to take two?"

He glared as if he wanted to pick me up and carry me away to the land of milk and honey. Although it touched my heart, making up at the start of praise break was out of order. He was distracting me in my line of duty and I needed him to go back to his seat. I hugged him and then nudged him to the side. I had to prepare for the final words and benediction.

⸙ Olivia blew a kiss from where she stood. All those sentimental meetings that consisted of holding hands, praying together, and laughing at her past antics were genuine. We both started the water works simultaneously. Her tears signified love and happiness. My tears signified relief and assurance.

I picked up the anointing oil beside the podium and skipped around the church, splattering liquid on everyone's forehead. I went into apostolic beast mode, giving everyone a piece of God's power that I had all over me.

I could have laid on the floor in God's presence all night; that's how much the service moved me. God spoke to me personally through his word and I received it. It was good to lay down all my burdens right there on the altar.

However, all things must come to an end and it was time for the benediction. I commanded the audience to lift their hands.

"May grace, mercy, and peace follow you all throughout the week. Amen?"

The crowd stood up, looking drained from being in God's presence and answered with a mediocre, "Amen."

I looked over at Olivia as she mouthed, "I'm proud of you, sweet baby."

Is the drama really suppressed now? Will we be one big happy family?

"Oh, and one more thing, church, before you go." Everyone jolted in place, anxious to hear what I had to say. "We have a visitor that I would like to acknowledge."

Daddy moved his head back and forth, looking around for my mystery guest.

"My biological mother, Olivia Wallace, is in the house of Mt. Zion. Let's show her some love before we leave out."

Daddy's eyes twitched, jerking over at Olivia. His deep voice echoed all throughout the building with everyone gawking at the pulpit.

At the top of his lungs, he shouted, "*You gotta be kidding me!*"

PASTOR JONES

CHAPTER 10

Five Years Ago...

"What is wrong with you, gal?"

Michelle laughed like a hyena escaping out of the wild. "Pastor, I feel good. I feel really good."

My mouth dropped. I just knew that my counseling techniques were working. She seemed so happy just the week before. What was going on now?

"Do we need to reschedule your appointment? You look high."

Her eyes were magnified as she stumbled closer. She moved her hands from side to side as if she was dancing with the devil. Whatever beat she heard in her head, it was playing a fast tempo with her feet fumbling across the office rug.

"Do you hear me talking to you, gal?"

I stared at her long and hard. She leaned up against the bookshelf with her eyes closed.

I commanded, pointing my finger at the nearest chair, "Sit down now, gal. I can't talk to you like this. Did you drive yourself here like this?"

"Yep." She grinned.

"My Father God." I winced.

"HELP ME," she whined.

I hissed, not knowing what to do next. "Lord have mercy. Let us pray, chile."

She started to hallucinate, calling me names as her childhood resurfaced in front of me. She swung at the air, becoming combative with the wind.

"Who are you fighting, gal? Calm down now."

"Get away from me. Stop it. Let me go!" she yelled to her invisible demons that attacked her. Within seconds, she fell to her knees and cried, "Lord, please help me. Please, somebody please help me."

All I could do was get down on the floor with her and rock. It was a moment I will never forget. I felt just as hopeless as she did as we cried together. Her mind rolled around in a maze trying to find its way to the nearest exit. The problem was at that moment, there wasn't one.

I sniffled, thinking about that night while standing outside the construction site of the church. After that night, I fought even harder to keep Michelle clean. It made me realize that although I thought I could fix anything and everything with God's anointing, I really wasn't in control of anything, only God was.

From group sessions, a psychologist, to rehab, she tried it and I didn't mind paying for it. I never gave up on her. I truly believed that God had an anchor that would soon allow her to stand on his word. Her father really messed her up and it was going to take years of therapy and prayer before she could fully recover.

"God didn't create anyone that he couldn't handle," Mother Smithfield said, giving a lopsided grin.

"Huh?" I sniffled again, now back from memory lane.

"What's ailing you, Cepheus? Who got you so sad lately? God can handle them, that's for sure."

"Is it that obvious, Mother?" I said, glancing at Habitat for Humanity, hammering down on the roof of the church.

"It's obvious, chile." Mother Smithfield shook my arm while standing beside me.

I moaned, "I'll be alright, I guess."

She looked up at the workers, trying to change the subject. "They working fast, aren't they? We'll be back in our beautiful church in no time."

"Yes, Ma'am, we sure will. Did I tell you about the new floor they added?"

"No, you didn't. What we need that for?"

I pointed to the top of the building. "It's for a homeless shelter. My own personal way of giving back."

"Look at you. That's alright right there."

My eyes became misty. "I remember my mother telling me to be good to the people. So that's what I'm trying to do. I need to make up for my disobedience to God with a sincere and opened heart for his people." I wiped my eyes. "I shole do miss that woman."

Mother looked away. "Yeah, I do too." Her false teeth chattered while attempting to speak clearly. Our eyes met, and she said, "Whatever is going on with you…this too shall pass."

She could probably feel that something wasn't right. She had a mother's intuition. She looked back up at me with an apologetic face. "Don't worry, Henry. I will do all I can to protect you. Whatever it is, I'm here if you need to talk."

"It's not something I want to talk about right now, Mother."

She shuffled the rocks around with her cane. "Well, if it's any consolation, I already know. I hear all the rumors going around. You know I get stuff from folks first hand."

"Boy, don't I know it." I chuckled.

"Well, if it'll make you feel better, I talked to the board and we want you back."

What?

My eyes watered. I was not expecting her to say that. *Just what I prayed for.*

"Yes, Ma'am."

"Now, listen, if I put you back, you need to get it right. I mean it."

"Yes, Ma'am."

"I believe in you and I will help you through this. But don't you dare touch another dime of the churches money to help you through your personal problems. Understood?"

"But..."

"You heard me, son. Paying Olivia all that money is one promise you can't keep." She sighed.

I exhaled, putting my hands over my face.

Mother continued, "Heck, give her a dollar a day like they do them African children on the PBS commercials. I bet you, she'll take whatever you give her. If you would have never signed your name to that silly contract, this wouldn't be an issue to start with." She snickered.

"I know."

"Lord have mercy, when that gal showed up for church on Sunday, I almost passed out."

"You and me both, Mother."

She looked away in disgust. "Don't you worry about her. You got to keep your eyes lifted to God. You hear me, son?"

I nodded. "Yes, Ma'am."

I put my arm around her shoulder for a quick mother and

son moment. She leaned into my chest, putting one arm around my back, hugging me tightly. She was getting soft in her old age, or at least when it came to dealing with me.

"What would I do without you, Mother?"

"Live, boy. 'Cause you can't do nothing for the dead. He-he."

Her laugh was infectious. I couldn't help but to join her. "Yes, Ma'am."

"It's time out for foolishness. You gotta clean house, son, and that means start with your own. Jesus is coming back real soon. Don't you want to be ready?"

"Yes, Ma'am, I do."

"Well, good, because I would hate to leave you behind."

Her shoulders bounced as she coughed and laughed all in one.

"You need to have one of those *come to Jesus* meetings like your mama used to have back in the day whenever you and your brothers were out of control. You need to do the same with your daughter and all those other gals you've claimed as children."

"Hmm." I grabbed my beard, nodding.

"Clear the air and let everyone know Pastor Henry Cepheus Jones is back!" She looked at me with a stern look. "It's time out for playing church, boy."

Yes, it is, Mother. Well, well, well. It's about that time.

NATALIA

CHAPTER 11

Pastor Jones called for a family meeting at the prison, to include Michelle. Mother Smithfield and my dad tagged along to give him support. While waiting in the visitation area, we prayed and then Pastor laid down the ground rules.

He cleared his throat.

"Here are the rules for today's gathering: No overacting, no dramatic scenes, no running off, no lies, and no shouting at each other. Got it? We are here to clear the air and become a civilized family once again. Okay?"

"Okay."

"This is wonderful, Pastor. I'm glad you're doing this," Beanie said, eyeballing Missy. "God will fix this. I know he will."

I caught myself wanting to get in his amen corner because I knew he was referring to Missy's odd behavior, but I remained quiet.

Frank shook his head at Missy while watching her swing a

handmade tear cloth back and forth.

"What is wrong with her?" he whispered in my ear.

I shrugged my shoulders. I was too busy playing with Micah and wasn't paying her any mind.

We all looked up as Michelle walked out of the steel doors. Her orange pants were sagging, and her hands flopped in front of her. She moved towards the table without saying a word.

"Hello, gal," Pastor mumbled.

"Hi, everyone." She gave a half wave.

Her eyes were glossy, and her speech sounded slurred. I knew that look from anywhere.

Is she high?

I've always heard of horror stories about narcotics being smuggled into prisons, but I'd never witnessed it. *Black Girls Reign* had a chat session awhile back, enlightening the team on how guards smuggle drugs by swallowing, stuffing it in balloons, stashing it in their jacket linings, or throwing bags of dope over the prison fence. It was then we realized that drugs were easier to access in the prison system than on the streets. I wasn't surprised that Michelle got ahold to some.

"Hey, gal. You ready to hold this heavy-headed boy?" Pastor asked, grabbing the baby out of my hands and lifting him up in the air.

She couldn't look at him, waving him away. "Nah, Natalia

can hold him. I'm a little tired today."

Pastor moved to the left, shoving Micah back into my arms.

"Is something wrong?" First Lady questioned, watching Michelle's body gestures.

"No," Michelle snapped, rolling her eyes.

Mother Smithfield leaned on her cane and said softly, "Lord have mercy. Is that gal *high*?"

Pastor pulled a mini notepad out of his pocket, refusing to acknowledge what was going on with Michelle. He started with a monotone voice. "Now, let me say this, I blame myself for all of the chaos in this here family. I wasn't a good role model as a father, or as a pastor and I'm sorry. I strive to do much better in the future because when I slack, y'all seem to follow suit."

I bounced Micah up and down, trying to keep him calm as he kept reaching for his mother. "I don't know what you're talking about, Pastor. I have enjoyed your leadership over the years. I don't see a problem at all."

"Suck up. Says the girl that hardly comes to church," Missy reeled.

The old Natalia was soon to be reincarnated. I had to catch my breath before speaking. I pushed the cursing demon down to my feet and said, "Good observation, Pastor Missy."

What I really had in mind was to stick my middle finger up at her while Pastor wasn't looking.

Pastor looked around the table with a serious face. "From here on out, I'm working on pleasing God first, which I hope will trickle down to all of you."

"Amen." Mother Smithfield looked over with pride, tapping her cane on the floor.

"I will also return every penny back to the church. For those of you that don't know. I stole money to pay back Olivia, although she never received any of it. I might as well confess to my family first before you hear it out there in the streets."

I put my head down, wishing he didn't just say that in front of everyone. I didn't like envisioning Pastor doing any wrongdoing, much less being a thief. He did a great job walking the walk and talking the talk. I understood why it had to be said, he was human...but still.

"Does anyone have anything they would like to add during our *clear the air* session, or as Big Mama used to say...our *come to Jesus* meeting?" he asked.

Michelle interjected slowly with her eyes half-closed. "I just want to say I'm sorry for all the trouble I've caused everyone. I'm not fit to be considered family, but I'm asking for your forgiveness."

I reached over to hug her with Micah in between us. "It's okay, sis. We love you and we forgive you," I said with enthusiasm, trying to brighten her spirits.

"Oh, so you're speaking for the entire table now?" Missy doubled back.

Mother Smithfield snapped back. "Lord have mercy, gal. You are beyond foolish sometimes."

Missy leaned over, shocked at Mother's words. It wasn't often that Mother would say something against the prized preaching machine.

"Do you have anything positive to say, gal?" Mother Smithfield asked with an inquisitive look.

"Why would I? I'm good," she answered.

Pastor Jones looked disappointed by his daughter's snooty behavior. "I can't wait for you to grow up, gal."

"I'm just saying…was this supposed to be therapeutic for all of us? I'm not getting anything out of this."

Beanie cut her off and said, "Missy's been suffering from migraines lately. I guess that medication got you cranky, huh, babe?"

She waved him off without a response.

I blew my breath now, wanting a piece of her face balled up in the palm of my hands. She was beyond rude for someone so anointed when in the pulpit.

Mother Smithfield rocked back and forth talking under her breath. "She need a swift butt whoopin', that's all."

I spoke up with a bubbly tone, attempting to ease the

tension at the table. "Okay, I'm next, right? I'm proud to say that I'm saved, sanctified, and filled with the Holy Ghost. And just because you don't see me at Mt. Zion, doesn't mean I'm not attending church. I'm going to church with my fiancé now."

"Fiancé?" Missy scoffed.

"Yes, my fiancé. We are attending church at Ebenezer Lighthouse."

"Why?"

"To get away from mixed emotional preachers like you, Missy, that's why."

She put her head down as I flared my fingers out in front of everyone to show off my new ring.

"Your fiancé, huh?" Mother Smithfield leaned forward to stare at the large multi-stoned cluster. "Well, hello, fiancé." She waved at Frank, twinkling her fingers as he waved back.

"Yes, it's official. We're engaged."

"Well, isn't that something. You didn't tell me this, gal. Congratulations. That's the church my brothers attend, ya know." Pastor beamed at the ring as if he had something to do with our union.

"Really?" I asked.

"Yep. We can talk about that another day," he hissed.

With the snippet of positive news, the conversation lightened up a bit. We started to enjoy one another's presence by just catching up on life in general. There were lots of smiles, plenty of laughter, and several hugs back and forth. Missy put away the tear cloth and soon realized it was not needed for this occasion. Michelle perked up as the drugs seemed to wear off. Mother Smithfield bragged about her last bingo game winnings. My dad sat back in chill mode, not mumbling a word. Beanie leaned back relaxed with his wide smile and hands folded. Frank snuggled up close, holding onto my shoulders the entire meeting. Baby Micah switched from lap to lap, bouncing around with his baby talk as his curly hair shimmered in the light. God was moving on our behalf. Maybe this corny therapeutic exercise was working after all.

Close to the end of the visit, Pastor said, "I hope this meeting helped, children."

"Yes," everyone replied.

"Well, good. When Michelle is released, we will resume these kinds of meetings on a regular basis. Amen?"

We spit out, "Amen," all at once.

"Alright. This concludes the first official *clear the air* slash *come to Jesus* meeting." He made quotation marks with his hands.

"Love it!" I cheered, joyfully leaning down to hug Michelle and kissing her on the cheek. In a few weeks, she would be returning to the real world. If I had anything to do with it, her first stop would be rehab.

MICHELLE

CHAPTER 12

ᴊᴋ"My name is Michelle Hanks and I'm an addict."

"Hi, Michelle," the group reeled back.

"Michelle, tell us a little bit about yourself." A white man with sandy brown hair sat in the middle of the U-shaped formation of chairs. He was apparently the ring leader of this group called *Restoration* for recovering drug addicts.

I didn't even get a chance to see Micah once I was released. Natalia drove me straight to the nearest rehab center where I would remain for the next three weeks.

"I'd rather not share any information right now," I answered with a serious face.

"We are here to help you, Ms. Hanks. We're all here for the same reason. Since you won't share your story, let me share mine." He coughed as if he was getting his throat clear for a long and drawn explanation of how he became clean.

"Let me introduce myself. My name is Harry and I'm an

addict."

"Hi, Harry," the group said with an upbeat voice.

"I was a veteran that fought for two wars and when I came back to my family, my wife of fifteen years left me for another man. I came home to a vacant house with a *for sale* sign in front of it. I moved here to North Carolina with my wife, because she transferred with her job. So, I requested to be stationed in the area. While I worked at Ft. Bragg in Fayetteville, she worked as a technical analyst at KForce Technology. I had no family here and no one to turn to once she decided to pick up and leave me for another man."

I didn't look up but listened attentively to his story.

"It was the worst day of my life to come back to an empty place that was once filled with love and laughter. The level of betrayal could have made me go postal. But, instead of taking my problems out on others, I found my own comfort...I turned to drugs."

I nodded, full of understanding.

"You see, Ms. Hanks, everyone has a story to tell and there is no need to feel ashamed of your personal experiences. Talking about it with people that have similar stories will eventually help you."

"I'm not ready for that just yet."

My first day out of jail and now I'm being pressured to tell my story?

Not.

When I finally looked up to view the faces that stared over at me, I saw nothing but smiles. I had no other choice but to sit and listen or else *Black Girls Reign* would shun me from the group. Not only did Natalia want me clean and sober before getting my baby, but she wanted me to be back to normalcy. Her memories of how I was as a teenager lingered, but yet in my mind, faded eons ago. She called me the free-spirited one. I wasn't free by any means, more bound than anyone around me. But, I knew how to conduct myself while around others and that made the difference. At this point, I didn't want to let anyone else down. I had to get it right for Natalia, *Black Girls Reign*, Pastor Jones, and especially Micah. I just had to.

A hand tapped my shoulder and said, "We are here for you, Ms. Hanks. You are now part of our family."

Family?

I doubled back, "Y'all act like drug addiction is like getting rid of a common cold. In my opinion, it's not that easy as you make it seem."

Harry crossed his legs and spoke calmly. "Oh, we never said this would be an easy task. It's very difficult to stay clean for anyone that has an addiction. But, one thing is for sure, you have come to the right place. Not only do we stick together, but we also remind one another why we're here. We all have loved ones awaiting our recovery."

True.

I closed my eyes, hoping to blink away the sight of these strange and peculiar people. But instead, they sat attentively waiting for my response.

I shook my head back and forth. "Maybe tomorrow."

"Very well then. We'll go around the room and allow others to speak." Harry carried on as if he had been doing this session all his life.

I soaked in all the other stories of twelve men and women that reminisced down the rocky road of drug abuse. From death, to molestation, to rape, and even murder. I realized I wasn't alone. There were so many others right in this room just like me.

By the end of the session, Harry gazed around the room and said, "Repeat after me." He paused, "We are powerless on our own and each day we will take personal inventory for one another as we fight our way to a drug-free life."

Everyone repeated after him as commanded while I sat mute, but yet silently elated about my freedom. I was only concerned about sniffing flowers, instead of being overwhelmed by the stench of musty women and urine-filled floors. Eating a pack of Oreo cookies to myself, while enjoying a glass of unspoiled milk would be rewarding right about now. Putting on clothes that would accentuate my curves and not make me look fifteen pounds heavier due to baggy and sagging pants would also be a plus.

I was home. I was finally home.

Telling my story was the last thing on my mind. All I wanted was to walk gingerly into the sunset, lift my head up to the stars and count them one by one, admiring the timeless movements of the clouds. I would go through the motions of rehab because it was expected of me. But, it was no guarantee that I could end my fixations of getting high.

PASTOR JONES

CHAPTER 13

Two Months Later.

Michelle had been released for several weeks before picking up Micah. She wanted to make sure she had all her ducks in order before taking full responsibility as his caregiver and biological mother. She came by the house in an Uber car that waited outside in the driveway. She walked into my home, going straight to the love seat next to the disco lamp, and waited patiently for her precious toddler.

Tonya motioned slowly around the house, gathering up his things with a wet face. I assisted, filling up the large trash bags full of toys, clothes, and baby shoes. It seemed as if she bought something for Micah every other day in current and future sizes. We had more than enough items to pack and give to his mother. One thing was for sure, he had enough items that would last him up until preschool.

"Please, Henry, don't let him go with her," she cried.

"Tonya, she gave birth to that boy and who are we to say she can't take him? We don't have any documentation that states he can't go with his mother, so stop all of this."

"Where is she taking him? Where will they stay?"

I turned towards her, holding down her flaring arms. "All of that is none of our business, Tonya. They'll be alright. You wait and see. Michelle wouldn't do anything to put that boy in harm's way. I know she won't."

She looked up with a pitiful look. "So, you're gonna just let him walk out of our lives just like that, Henry?"

"Stop with all that yap. You act like the boy is moving to Alaska. Now, hurry up and finish bagging up all of his stuff so that gal can live happily ever after. She deserves a happy ever after, Tonya."

She leaned against the wall and said, "What about me being happily ever after?"

"You'll have to find something else that will fill your void, honey, because he's going back with her, whether you like it or not."

She turned away with disgust. Several trash bags later, I handed them over to the woman whom he would eventually call *mama*.

Micah became a handful since he started walking. Which made this detachment a breeze for me and I didn't have a problem with his departure. I was glad to see Speedy Gonzalez go far from here, because I was too old to be chasing his rambunctious little behind around the house.

Michelle ignored everything around her, spinning Micah around in the air and making him laugh uncontrollably.

I grabbed Tonya's hand as she continued to cry. "It's going to be okay. It really is. You will get through this."

I shoved her head onto my chest. All I could hear was muffled words. "I love him, Henry. I love that boy."

"I know you do, honey. Maybe we can adopt one day if we need to. Will that help?"

"*No.*"

With sarcasm, I answered, "Well, pray about it. I bet if you start coming to church and giving God some of your time, instead of all those clothing boutiques, nail salons, and massage parlors, you might get blessed with a child."

Tonya stopped acting like a First Lady when she exchanged words with Missy a few years back. Since then, she decided not to step foot back into Mt. Zion, unless it was for a special occasion. I was certain that a shopping spree at Nordstrom's would ease her pain within the next few days. I hoped this was just a phase and she would eventually get back to her normal nonchalant self.

"You ready, Michelle?" I walked back to the living room,

moving trash bags from the back.

"Yep." Michelle turned to Tonya, giving a fake smile. "Thanks for everything, First Lady."

We walked up to the Uber vehicle, stuffing bags inside the trunk. Little Micah reached his arms out, looking at Tonya.

Michelle rolled her eyes, putting Micah in a yellow and black car seat. As she looked back at us, she looked down, squeezing his cheeks and said, "No need to reach for her anymore, son. I'm your real mama." She pointed back at Tonya and said, "That lady over there is now your auntie. Say auntie?"

Tonya rushed to my arms and broke down.

Michelle jumped in on the passenger side and rolled down the window with the car in motion.

"Thanks for everything, Pastor Jones." She blew a kiss and rolled the window back up. We stood there watching the Jeep until it left our sight.

We were blessed to have a pinch of joy in our home for such a short period of time. Having him around definitely sparked more conversations, created family moments, and made us appreciate one another through the parenting process. But now that Micah was gone, it was back to doing what we used to do before he came into our lives as a married couple, which was *nothing.*

PASTOR JONES

CHAPTER 14

The following day I met with the board down at the church. It was a unanimous vote to swear me back in as the head board member.

It was time to get back to church business. The *new* church was complete, and we had several topics to discuss pertaining to cost, materials, and furniture. Our meeting was held in a newly designed board room area with several new amenities. The new space was five times the size of the last one with a big screen television in the center of the room. The aroma of the new area was breathtaking and hit our noses as soon as we walked in.

The smell of apple cider wood chips, freshly coated paint, and lavender air freshener lingered down the hallways. When I entered the office, I opened the venetian blinds that hung from the new spacious windows to get a bit of natural light to beam into the room. The magnificent view of the water fountains in the walkway was breathtaking as water splashed up, pouring tiny sprinkles around it. I was proud of the new and improved.

Maybe the burning down of our building was a blessing after all and not so much of a curse as I once thought.

"Alrighty, let's begin. The homeless shelter and soup kitchen are now operating at full capacity, with community volunteers on deck. How are we going to handle the grand opening?"

"I say we invite community leaders, Mayor Steve Schewel, and Bill Bell since he gave us the keys to the city," Mother Smithfield said.

"I agree," Deacon Freemon concurred.

"And before we go any further, I just want to say thanks to the board for allowing me back to work with this wonderful team."

\The board members glanced over with half-smiles.

"Good to have you back, Passuh. You've been missed." Mother Smithfield winked in my direction.

"Alright, on another note. I've returned some of the money I borrowed last year. The rest of the funds should be replaced by the end of this fiscal quarter."

"Oh, how nice," Mother Gaines chimed in.

Missy sat at the far end of the table, disengaged. Her Apple watch had her undivided attention and she didn't look up not once.

Sister Mary pulled out an array of colored pens to take

notes, while staring stupidly with a love-struck glare at Deacon Freemon.

"The donations from the prayer cloths that we sold during commercial breaks are helping out a lot." I set my hands on my belly, leaning back.

Everyone sat quietly with their hands folded in front of them.

"Let's change the subject and talk about the painting needed for the other rooms inside the church. We hear you, Passuh, about the returned money. Now back to painting," Mother Agnes said.

"I agree we have a lot of painting to do, especially upstairs. It's another winter season and we have several individuals taking advantage of the shelter facility. We'll have to paint in the early mornings when most of them go out to work or looking for jobs," Mother Smithfield said.

"I know, right?" Sister Mary said, looking up with bright eyes.

"So far, we have housed fifteen people, one of which goes by the name of Olivia Wallace." Mother Smithfield looked away in disgust.

The board members looked at me and then over at Missy.

Mother Smithfield continued, "Yes, I know what y'all are thinking, folks. But Passuh, Missy begged me to approve her stay. I have nothing to do with this preposterous decision."

I moaned, "Uh-huh. Why didn't you inform us before this meeting, Missy? I think we should've all been included with the decision making of who gets a bed and who doesn't, don't you think?"

Missy continued to look down at her watch.

Mother Smithfield interjected in defense, "I made a decision based upon Passuh Missy's plea. Trust me, I don't want her here either."

"Why is she here?"

"Why don't you ask her?" She pointed to Missy. "She's been the HNIC, the Head Negro in Charge of this operation since you've been gone."

"Okay, HNIC. Why in the world would you allow this?" I muttered, ogling her down.

"Listen, she's in a real bad state right now. She needed this," Missy answered without making any eye contact.

"I don't care what state she's in. She's dangerous!" I was in a rage as I found myself raising my voice and slapping my hand down on the table.

Missy rolled her eyes, unalarmed. "God is still in the miracle business, Daddy. She's not the same as before. God can change anyone. He changed you, right?"

"That demon you're protecting can't be fixed, Missy."

"Don't you dare compare your father's change to what she needs," Mother Smithfield spouted.

"I agree totally, Mother," I stuttered with disbelief.

Missy huffed. "She's given up the fight for your money. Trust me on this one."

"And you believe her? You believe the arsonist of this here church that cost us millions to rebuild has changed? Are you serious right now, Missy? Ashton Kutcher must be up under this table with a camera. What's the name of that show that used to come on cable?" I put my finger up to my head thinking.

"You mean *Punk'd*?" Sister Mary implied.

"Yes. That's exactly it, *Punk'd*. Right now, Missy, that is what's going on. You're being *Punk'd* by the crack head con artist."

"Daddy, you'll have to see it for yourself to believe what I'm saying."

I pushed my chair out and stood up to the challenge. "Doggonit. Let's go right now, then." I rushed out the door and marched straight up the back stairs without looking back. Missy followed right behind me.

Each step I took, I mouthed words, feeling flustered.

"She's not staying here, I tell you that."

"Yes, she is," Missy hissed, shaking her finger in the air.

"Over my dead body."

She looked up as if she was thinking to herself, *die then, fool.*

"You're the last thing she's thinking about, Daddy. Let her be."

We entered the spacious front forum of the shelter. We walked back into the bed area, opening a wide door. Olivia laid in the first bed. I stopped dead in my tracks as our eyes connected.

She looked like a decrepit senior citizen holding on to the thin bed covers. Next to her hip was a plastic container that resembled a catheter. It flapped over her hip as her fragile body turned to the side, trying to hide it. She had a rosy undertone all over her skin, barely sitting up on her elbows.

You gotta be kidding me.

She was so sickly looking that I was convinced she had that manmade disease.

I stood back, leaning over into Missy's ear. "Does she have the...*pluck?*"

Missy looked back, baffled. "Huh?"

"That disease with the four capital letters."

Missy put her hands over her mouth. "Really? Did you just ask that with her sitting right in front of us?"

I shrugged my shoulders. "Olivia, what's wrong with you, gal?"

Olivia spoke softly with her Eartha Kitt voice. "So nice to see you too, Henry."

"What the hell happened to you, woman?"

"I'm dying."

"You don't say. Dying of what?" I stared at her scaly feet.

"If you must know, I have cancer."

Missy grabbed her hand for comfort as soon as the "C" word came out.

"How long has this been going on?"

"Why does that matter, Henry?"

"You're a liar and the truth just ain't in ya, that's why. Missy, you believe this mess?"

"Daddy?"

I snickered. "Unbelievable. You're laying up in here pretending to die so you can get Missy's attention. Shame on you, woman. Such a cheap trick."

Missy was mortified. "Please excuse my heartless father. Can't you just forgive her and move on?"

"H…to the nah to the nah, nah, nah. I can't forgive that witch. Have you lost your cotton pickin' mind, gal? You know she's putting on an act, right?" I waited for an answer.
"Don't you?" I was disgruntled and wanted to snatch Olivia out of that bed ASAP.

Missy ignored me, looking over at the actress and asked,

"Have you taken anything for pain today?"

"Oh, chile, the pain is so often that I don't even bother anymore." She reached for Missy's other hand.

"So, now you two are kissy-kissy, huh?"

"I trust her completely, Daddy. I went to visit her in prison on several occasions. She's realized her faults, and all is forgiven." Missy cracked a smile, mesmerized by her mother's sob story.

I looked at both of them cross-eyed. "I swear I must be in the twilight zone for real. Missy, I raised you better than this. Use your discernment, gal. It's a hoax!"

Olivia moaned in pain.

"Lawd have mercy. Stop with all that fake noise. Get up out that bed so someone that really needs it can use it."

"Daddy!"

"Don't 'Daddy' me." I moved the covers off her legs, while Missy was on the other side of the bed, putting them back on her.

I stood in pure shock.

"You gonna pray for her, Daddy?"

"What did you just ask me?"

Missy grabbed her hand. "Father God…"

She moaned in pain after every word.

This was one prayer I didn't want to be a part of. I stepped back, folding my arms.

"Amen," Missy squealed.

Olivia blinked her eyes in response, giving nonverbal *I love you* cues. Without hesitation, Missy sat in the chair beside her. Her eyes gave the peace sign while holding on to Olivia's thin hands. They clutched one another tightly.

Olivia sobbed loudly and said, "Know that I love you with all of my heart, daughter."

"It's okay, Olivia. I know you do. I love you too."

"What the Sam Hill…I can't take no more of this foolishness." I stormed out of the room, shaking my head back and forth. My heart was leaping up and down in my chest. My daughter had all this Holy Ghost power, yet couldn't discern the devil's imp when laying right there in front of her.

That gal's mind is gone. It's time for her to take several seats from pastoring. She's gone completely cray-cray.

NATALIA

CHAPTER 15

It was only a few hours until our guest arrived for the annual Christmas dinner. I cooked up a storm for the family which included: pound cake, fried chicken, red velvet cake, peach cobbler, sweet potato pies, baked macaroni, collard greens, broccoli casserole, mashed potatoes, and a well-seasoned fried turkey. Frank's famous sherbet punch was also bubbling in the punch bowl, with ginger ale fuzzing at the top. It was beginning to look a lot like Christmas as our seven-foot artificial tree glistened with Panther-themed decorations. It was vibrant, sitting in front of the living room window and could be seen from the outside.

Frank loved helping me in the kitchen and sampled everything piled up on the kitchen counter. He wanted to make sure that each item was seasoned to perfection as he was used to. His Henderson upbringing made him an expert.

We invited everyone not only to eat our delicious meal, but also to share our exciting news. We eloped a few days prior and I was ecstatic being Frank's one and only *wifey*. We honored God and united as one. I wasn't the beautiful bride I anticipated on being, but I was happy and that's all that mattered to me now.

Being officially married came with benefits. I didn't have to fight the urge of taking him to the bedroom. And, on that note, it was on like popcorn, I attacked him every chance I could get. I had the privilege of touching every part of his body without feeling ashamed. One thing for sure, we made up for lost time.

It was a good thing I didn't have any chandeliers hanging in our home. I could see myself swinging on one of them after all this good loving and it was a horrible accident waiting to happen. From the kitchen, to the floor, to the living room and the bathroom, marriage allowed us free reign to sanction every piece of furniture in our home. Such a beautiful ordination by God and we enjoyed every minute of it.

I licked the cake filling off the tips of my fingers and said, "This is going to be the best Christmas ever."

"You think so?" Frank asked.

"Of course, it is! I'm married to one of the most handsome men in North Carolina. My dad has settled down with one woman that he said I would soon meet. Michelle is finally home. Missy has calmed herself all the way down, and Pastor is handling his business like never before. Yes, this is definitely the best Christmas I've ever witnessed in all of my twenty-nine years of living."

"Well, just keep that jovial spirit when everyone piles in within the next few minutes. We have a surprise guest coming."

I swung my head around. "Who?"

He grinned, kissing me dead in the mouth. "You sure you want to know?"

"I'm sure. Spill it, handsome."

"Missy is bringing her mother with her."

"What do you mean? Missy's mother died years ago."

"No, I mean the woman who gave birth to her, not the woman who raised her."

I dropped my spoon in the middle of the floor as cake batter splattered onto my slippers. "SAY WHAT?"

"Pastor Jones called, giving me the heads up this morning. I thought I should warn you."

I spun my neck around quickly. "Why didn't you tell him to drive her to the nearest gutter and dump her trifling behind right there? Why is she coming here?"

"I don't think she'll be a problem."

❧ I picked up the spoon, talking rapidly, "I just talked to Missy last night and she didn't mention anything about that ratchet woman. Not one time. Mercy."

He coughed, trying hard to hold in laughter. "All I can say is fix your pretty face while she's here. Give her that southern charm that I've seen a million times before when we had guests."

Southern charm for Olivia? Lord, help us all.

My sassy tone erupted and shot out my mouth. "As long as she doesn't come for me, I won't come for her."

"I doubt you'll have any problems, Nat. Chill out."

"Oh? How so?"

"She has stage-four cancer."

Is it really cancer or the pluck?

I moved around the kitchen in silence wondering if I should add bleach to Olivia's drink or douse her with acid. Just when I thought this was going to be the best Christmas ever, the devil poked his ugly little head up from the ground and rained on my parade.

The doorbell rang. Frank rushed to answer as I pulled out the silverware and placed it on top of the red and black place settings. I rushed around, making things tidy, as Frank turned the front doorknob to let everyone in. We were able to seat ten people in the dining area and four more in the kitchen if necessary. I exhaled, wiping my hands on my "Divas are born in February" apron. I was not in the mood for nonsense and a full bottle of bleach was on standby.

"Well, hello, beautiful people. *Merry Christmas.* Come on in and make yourself at home." Frank stood at the front door with a welcoming grin, watching everyone walk in one by one.

"Yeah, hello, everyone. Come on in." My face felt like it was going to crack in half if I smiled any harder. I stood in place with open arms, grabbing coats and piling them up on the sofa. Everyone entered that was considered family along with the woman I did not want to see. Olivia Wallace came through the doors of my new home, making her grandiose appearance.

I put my hands over my mouth, scanning her bony body as Missy rolled her in with a wheelchair. She was hunched over and looking thinner than a broomstick.

"Well, what a pleasant surprise. Nice to see you again."

I didn't respond.

I guess.

Frank hovered behind me, giving me the cue to speak. "Yes, glad you could join us and be part of our annual family dinner."

She sniffled. "Thanks. What's your name again?"

"N-A-T-A-L-I-A."

"Uh-huh. I got it now."

I wasn't completely sold on her illness, but she did look closer to death than life. It was an awkward moment for everyone as they stood in silence. Looking at her made me count my blessings as I put my hands together, praying silently. She was going to take her last breath sooner than later. I just hoped it wasn't during my magnificent Christmas dinner. Too much labor went into cooking all of this food. That was the last thing we needed around here. The fact that Missy was standing by her side being so supportive was even more confusing.

Frank broke the silence. "Alright, everyone, please have a seat. Let's get started."

The group shuffled around the room, looking for a seat. Once everyone settled, I stood in front of the dining room entrance and said, "Now that you're all comfy, Frank and I have something we want to share."

"What? Did y'all win the lotto?" Daddy laughed at his own statement, slapping his knee.

"I wish. Hold on to your hat, Daddy. You might like this one even better."

He shifted his Kangol hat towards the back of his head and said, "Better than winning the lotto?"

I rolled my eyes and shouted with energy and throwing my hands up in the air, "Frank and I are officially husband and wife!"

"Ayyyyeeeeee!" Michelle spouted.

"Yeah, that don't sound nothing like the lotto." Daddy snickered.

The body language of each individual after hearing the news was made for a reality television show. Daddy shuffled his hands around full of nervousness. Pastor Jones and First Lady Tonya clapped as if the Panthers had just won the Super Bowl. Missy snorkeled which came across as a mixture of choking and crying. Mother Smithfield giggled loudly as if she was Ms. Sophia from the *Color Purple*. Olivia raised her head up with a cold expression. Michelle rushed over, almost knocking me down and hugging and kissing me all around my cheeks with Micah in her hands. Then suddenly, it dawned on me. Someone was missing…Beanie? *I don't see Beanie.*

"Missy?"

"Yes."

"I just realized Beanie isn't here today. What's up?"

She didn't respond, grabbing a Chinet paper plate and digging into the peach cobbler that sat in the center of the dining room table. She scooped a pile of it onto her plate and blinked away the question.

"Hello? Earth to Missy Rochelle Jones."

She sampled a piece of the cobbler and sat down, not making any eye contact with anyone in the room. "It's obvious that he isn't here."

Frank huffed, looking tired of her attitude already and said, "Yes, it's very obvious."

Lord, did he finally leave the spoiled brat after all?

PART III

ANYTHING'S POSSIBLE

"And looking at them Jesus said to them, with people this is impossible, but with God all things are possible."

Matthew 19:26

MISSY

CHAPTER 16

A few weeks before the Christmas gathering, everything fell apart. I decided to hash out our differences in the office of my psychologist.

❧*The weather went from cold to hot again, messing up my sinuses. I walked in the front office of the psychology building with an excruciating, pounding headache. Beanie was making me feel miserable right after Thanksgiving. I couldn't take it anymore. It was just something about his annoying Jamaican accent that now made me want to trade him in for a newer model. I was deeper into the word now that Olivia was back in my life. It was the one thing that helped me to gain focus on my calling. I was missing a mother, but now I felt complete. The closer I walked with God, the less I cared about being with Beanie and dealing with his attitude and mood swings.*

I wanted to share my innermost feelings about the situation with Dr.

Brown. I had completely opened up during our sessions and I felt safe now, expressing my inner thoughts with him and him only. Taking Beanie with me and allowing him to listen to my thinking process would be best as I feared having such a life changing conversation alone.

We arrived at the psychologist's office on LaSalle Street. Beanie came inside and sat down in the lobby with his usual frown. The big cheesy smile he used to carry was nonexistent. His face was now molded to an unrecognizable permanent formation as if he hated my guts. While sitting in the waiting area, Dr. Brown stood at his office door and said, "Come in."

I walked in, ready to chatter about anything and everything under the sun. "Thanks, Dr. Brown."

"Always a pleasure." He walked to his seat and said, "What's going on, Missy?" He leaned back, tilting his brown boots with colorful Superman socks expanding outward.

I remained standing, looking over at all his collective coffee cups. He had a new one that wasn't on his desk the last time I came, that read, "Boys rule the world too." It was kind of feminine in my opinion, but he was considered one of those metrosexual kind of guys anyway, based upon the clear fingernail polish I noticed on his nails.

I spoke softly, "I can't go on like this, Doc. It's like I'm a new person and I don't need someone like Beanie dampening my spirit daily. Every second I'm around him, I cringe. I need to start my life all over again and regroup. It's about to be a brand-new year soon and it will be my year of full transformation. A new year, a new me."

His eyebrows caved in as if he had heard this liberation speech before. "So, you're finally finding yourself, huh?"

"I guess you can say that, Doc."

"That's what it sounds like. You're figuring out what makes Missy tick. That's a good thing. How does Beanie feel about this transformation?"

I shrugged my shoulders.

"Is he here with you today?"

I sat down, slowly inching back onto the brown sofa. I crossed my legs over one another, feeling more at ease than when I entered. "Yes, he's with me."

"So, what happens next now that you have found the real you?"

"I need some time alone."

Dr. Brown gave a skeptical glance. "Deep stuff. Are you sure you're ready for this sudden change of heart? Is the plan to break up with him in the presence of your psychologist?"

"Yep, that's the plan, Doc." I held my head down.

"Kind of cold, don't you think?"

"Yes, it was spineless and rude, but it's best I get rid of him before he gets rid of me. Got to save face somehow. It's easier to explain to church folks that I'm moving closer to God, than to tell them that I broke up with what they consider the most caring and loving man of my time."

"I see."

"Plus, I think the feelings are mutual."

"I think you're being melodramatic, Missy." Dr. Brown bounced his pencil on his cheek.

"You think?"

I didn't care about his formulated opinion. I talked over him, venting my side of the story and how things had gone sour between us. Fifteen minutes later, he looked up with weary eyes as if I had drained the life out of him. He cautiously buzzed into the front office to call Beanie in for his summons. I looked back at him, nodding my head to confirm that I was still alright with Beanie joining us.

"Sandra?"

"Yes, Dr. Brown?" she answered.

"In the next five minutes, please send Mr. Anderson in my office."

"Sure thing, Dr. Brown."

He looked back at me and said, "I personally don't agree with your approach on this matter, Missy. Your perception of things can be skewed at times. I feel you have a one-sided view of this relationship and you're not being fair to this man. I also feel you should think this thing out a little longer before doing this."

I looked back with a blank stare. "Why?"

"Well, you described him as being a man of high standards and you've boasted on the things he's done for you in the past." His eyebrows furrowed as he gave me a stare of disbelief.

"Trust me. It's the right thing to do. You don't understand."

"Trust me, I do understand." He fumbled with his pencil. *"Are you sure this isn't coming from a deep dark place from your past? I suggest the two of you take a vacation and talk this out."*

It dawned on me that Dr. Brown was feeling sorry for Beanie and could not have cared less about my feelings.

"Doc, I know what love is and I just don't feel it when it comes to Beanie anymore."

He paused. "Well, what is love to you, Missy?"

I became a culmination of my father as I started talking with my hands. "I don't get butterflies in my stomach when he walks by. I don't get starry eyed when I see him in a new outfit or smell his cologne lingering around the room. I don't get tingling sensations when he puts his arms around me. The bottom line is, he came into my life when I was at my worst. I'm better, stronger, wiser and I don't think it's a good idea to go from one bad relationship to the next." I paused, gulping the tears down.

"That's it? If that is all you know about love, then you don't know what love is, Missy." He scrunched his face.

"I'm not wifey material anyway, so yes, this breakup needs to happen."

Dr. Brown took notes as we both looked up at the knock on the door. "Come in."

Beanie poked his head in, swinging the door behind him. "The receptionist stated that you wanted to see me, Dr. Brown?"

"Yes, come on in, Beanie. Missy wanted you to join us. Come on in

and take a seat next to Missy, please." Dr. Brown rose from his seat, shaking Beanie's hand. I stretched my arms upward, preparing to give the ultimate let down.

It was too late to turn back now. I turned sideways and looked Beanie dead in his beautiful brown eyes. "Beanie, I wanted you to know that I'm striving to be a better person."

"Okay." He smiled.

"I realize that I come from a history of dysfunctional folks, but I'm determined to be different."

"Okay. What does that have to do with me?" He looked back with a wrinkled forehead.

"I want to be honest with you. Completely honest with you about everything."

He looked up at Dr. Brown and then back at me. "I'm listening."

"I love you. I think you're a wonderful person. You have a beautiful spirit inside and out. You make me laugh, you hold me close when I'm feeling bad, and I know you genuinely have my best interest at heart."

He blew out air with a look of wonder.

I didn't take my eyes off him and continued, "You have become a major help in my life. As a matter of fact, I wouldn't be back in counseling if it wasn't for you pushing me to do better for myself."

His face wrinkled up tighter as if he felt some bad news coming forth.

I grabbed his hand and said, "The truth is, Beanie, you came into my life at my weakest point. I don't want you to think that I don't love you *when I say this, but I don't want to keep stringing you along. You deserve better and I pulled you in here to say…"*

He snatched his hand back, slowly crossing his arms.

Dr. Brown leaned forward. "Missy, I think…"

I looked over, putting my hands up and feeling passionate about getting it all out. "It's okay, Dr. Brown. I'm a big girl. Let me finish my thoughts." I continued, "I do believe God puts people together for a reason and a season and quite frankly, our season ends today."

Beanie's eyes bulged. "Say what? You call yourself breaking up with me?" He looked as if he was just dehumanized in front of another man.

"Something like that."

"After all I've put up with?" A vein popped forth in his forehead as his eyes became misty.

I blinked several times, still looking eye to eye, and not moved by his words. "In order for me to be the Pastor that God has called me to be, I have to let you go."

Beanie's eyes were turning fiery red. "You selfish little…This is bull…" He kept catching himself, trying not to lose his cool.

Dr. Brown threw his hand up like a referee ending a verbal boxing match. "Alright, Missy, you drove your point home. Beanie, do you have something you would like to say to Missy?" Dr. Brown was giving him the look of bruh, please don't go out like this. Say something, please.

"What can I say to a selfish, money hungry, mental case like her?"

"Oh, so now I'm a mental case, Beanie?" I jumped to my feet, balling

up my fists, and pulling my sleeves up.

"Okay, let's settle down, people. Y'all just need a break from one another, that's all."

"Yeah, a permanent one," I lashed back.

"Are you serious right now, Missy?" Beanie moved off the sofa, marching closer to the door.

Dr. Brown looked down at his fancy watch, while Beanie looked back with pride oozing out of his eyes.

"I just felt I needed to be honest with you, Beanie. I don't want anyone to get hurt."

"I guess it's too late for that, huh?" He sighed.

"How about we meet back here next Thursday around the same time. Just take a couple of days away from one another and see how it goes," Dr. Brown pleaded.

Beanie walked out, slamming the door behind him. I could hear him yelling in the hallway. "You don't want a real man, Missy Jones! So, keep fantasizing about that dead man. Deuces."

Dr. Brown stood up with energy, shaking his head. "See, I told you I didn't think this was a good idea, Missy."

Tears rolled onto my neck. "It had to be done, Doc. It will all work out for my good."

———

I didn't go straight home after that visit. I couldn't face Beanie at the moment. I stopped at Starbucks on Roxboro Road and ordered a blonde latte with my Starbucks app. I needed some time alone. Coffee normally healed all wounds when I needed it to. I thought about what Dr. Brown said so eloquently; I was being *melodramatic*.

But, was I?

I arrived home hours later. No Beanie, no boxes, not even a toothbrush left behind. It didn't matter. I felt deep down in my soul that this was the right thing to do. I held my coffee in my hand, swishing around the sugar at the bottom. I could hear an echo when I gulped. The last remnant of my now lukewarm substance was gone, just like my Jamaican boyfriend.

Maybe I overreacted just a bit. But, it was time to check myself and I needed a break from a man. Numbness infused my body as I contemplated flopping on the sofa. Once upon a time, I needed a man to make me whole. But today, I felt empowered with just me, myself, and I…and God.

I was in a good place mentally and physically. My anxiety was minimal, my preaching had mainstreamed worldwide, and my faith was stronger than ever before. My sadness was now becoming my joy. All in all, God was turning it all around for me and I needed space for my own personal deliverance.

MICHELLE

CHAPTER 17

❧"I hate this place, Nat."

"Why, because you're required to stay sober?" Natalia asked, leaning back on her elbows and putting her feet up on the hard mattress of the queen-sized bed.

I wanted to roll my eyes, but instead I winced, knowing she was right on the money with that statement.

I needed a drink, a pill, a ball of shiny stuff…something to make me feel good about this situation.

I looked back at Nat with my peripheral.

"No answer, huh?" she sputtered with a vague look across the room.

My addictive spirit was brewing. I was disgusted at my current living situation. We may have been poor back in the day, but we never had rats, roaches, or bed bugs lurking around us. The conditions of the halfway house were unreal and yet, I was supposed to stay here with a child?

"This is only short-term, Michelle. Just stick it out until the girls can find a better fit for you."

"Well, how long will that take? By the time they find something suitable, the rats in here would have already chewed up Micah's feet."

"Listen, this was far away from the dope man and big enough for you to move around in. So, stop complaining. I would invite you to my crib, but we don't have any guest bedroom furniture yet."

"Hurry up and get some before I call Habitat for Humanity on this dump."

Calling it a dump was an understatement. The house was an old *Amityville Horror* lookalike, built in the 1800s. It was in the county section, going towards a small town called Bahama. It resembled a slave owner's home, with a backyard that seemed more than two miles long filled with tobacco leaves and cotton. There was a tiny outhouse on the left side of the structure that was still being utilized in present day, due to the horrible drainage in the inside. The renovations the owner claimed to have done were nonexistent as the smell of mildew assaulted my nose daily. To top it all off, the heating system was outdated, with woodstoves on each floor and piles of logs beside it. I felt like I was staring into the movie, *Roots*. The city should have bulldozed the house right after the Civil Rights Movement if you asked me.

"How many women live here anyway?" Natalia asked.

"Who knows. I stay in this room half the time. The smell alone keeps me wheezing around here."

Natalia looked around at the dust balls on the floor and the rat pellets by the window. "I see."

"Can't your little woman advocacy cheerleaders find me something else by the weekend?"

"After seeing rat poop, I will definitely push the issue tonight. I thought you were over-exaggerating when you called me. But yeah, this is a bit much for a child. She paused, "Has your mom come by to see you since you've been out?"

I leaned over on my elbow. "Not at all and I didn't expect her to either."

"Why you say that? I thought you and ma dukes were on good terms."

"Long story."

Natalia scooted back further on the bed. "Well, I'm listening." Her eyes fluttered. "Besides, you know I'm nosy. Spill the tea." She grabbed Micah out of my hands, bouncing him up and down as he laughed at his man-made bouncy. "Ain't that right, little man?"

"You don't even know the half, Nat."

"Well, what I do know is your family has a phenomenal rag to riches story for the Oprah Winfrey Network. Such a successful comeback, to be farmers that struck it big after all that hard labor and work over the years. People in this area go crazy over local farmer products lately. I can see why it became such a big lucrative industry so fast."

"Yep." I twiddled my fingers on my cheek.

"I always see your fine little brothers delivering stuff to that country store, Red and White, off Club Boulevard. Do you ever talk to them?"

"Nope."

"Huh?" She pondered. "Well, what about your dad? Is he still living?"

I wasn't in the mood for the debauchery of going down memory lane, especially with *his* son bouncing in the air looking just like him.

"I don't care to rehash stuff, Nat. Long story."

I looked away out the window behind the bed post.

"I see. Always remember, parenting doesn't come with a play by play handbook. So, I'm sure at the next family reunion, you all will be breaking bread together again as a family." She chuckled, trying to stay pleasant.

A touch of anger smeared across my face. "I doubt that very seriously."

She noticed the change in my mood. "Why are you looking like that?"

"I had a really bad childhood. Hurtful memories. Lots of tears behind it."

"I'm sorry. I didn't mean to upset you, sis. But, I remember the statement you made about your father at the restaurant while pregnant with Micah. Do you remember that?"

I flashed back to that day I met with Missy and Nat at the chicken and waffle restaurant. I said some stuff that I wouldn't normally say as I shared the details of my relationship with Tommy Lee Davis and the first pregnancy at age 14 with my father. I wished I had a magic wand that could erase that moment in time.

I blinked. "Somewhat."

"You said something about getting pregnant by your father at fourteen. Is that true? I thought you were full of lies back then, so I never asked to clarify."

I put my head down, slowly staying focused on the rat feces in order not to make eye contact. "Yes, it's true."

"Lawd. Let me call my husband and tell him to get the bail money ready. You know I can't stand hearing stuff like this."

I smirked, trying desperately to change the subject. "Look at you emphasize the phrase *my huzzz…banddd*. I never thought I'd hear those words come out of your mouth."

She blushed. "Yep, finally found me a lifetime, boo."

"How did you know he was the one?"

She rolled her eyes. "Girl, don't try to get me off track. What the heck happened with you and your father?"

I hesitated and then lowered my tone in shame. "He'd been molesting me for years, Nat. Nothing more to say."

"Did your mother know about this?"

"She never believed me until I got pregnant. Then, she blamed me for everything. Said I was being fast and tempted the man."

"Say what?"

"You asked. So now I'm sharing with you. After pouring my guts out to *Restoration* three times a week, sharing comes easier for me these days. I wasn't blessed to have the perfect childhood like you or Missy. I only wish my daddy loved me the way your fathers love on the two of you."

"Whew, chile! This explains everything." She sat, baffled.

"I guess it does."

"I'm so sorry, Michelle."

Her discernment kicked in high gear as she put her hand over her mouth, fishing for more details. "So, when was the last time you've seen him? Your father. What's his name?"

I became quiet, not wanting to recoil blow by blow.

"Andrew Hanks and you don't want to know."

She looked at me and then back at Micah and then back at me again.

"Oh, no, sis. Don't tell me..." Tears filled her eyes as her voice cracked with rage.

"I'm begging you, Nat. Don't ever share who Micah's father is with anyone. I don't mind telling my story about abuse and molestation, but I dare not share how Micah got here."

"I know. I know." She grabbed me and held me tightly.

"Why didn't your mother have him arrested?"

"Please. If Pastor Jones didn't find out about it, he would have stayed with her until death and she would've allowed the abuse to continue." I leaned back, taking a deep breath. "So, now you know all there is to know about your dear old friend, Michelle Hanks. I'm jacked up."

She doubled back, "Don't say that, sis. You are God's child and you will be a living testimony for others that have gone through this same thing one day. You wait and see."

I nodded my head. I knew her brain was churning, and I knew she was concocting a plan. It was either revenge, speaking engagements, or more counseling. She had something brewing in that genius leveled head of hers.

Seconds later, she spit out words with passion and authority. "We're going to find that bastard. He's going to pay for what he did to you. I will make sure of it."

"Natalia?"

"Don't 'Natalia' me. I will have to say this in my Oprah voice. His time is UP," she mimicked Oprah making her profound speech at the *Golden Globe Awards* concerning her new advocacy group created to protect women like me.

"Oh my. I can see you now on *CBS Good Morning,* sitting beside every woman and girl that came forth with a story like mine." I smirked.

"You better believe it."

Natalia's high volume of strength shifted into my distant soul. She empowered me as I said, teary-eyed, "I will get through this, Nat. I will try really hard to get through this."

She immediately jumped to her feet, picked up my things with one hand, and propped Micah on her hip with the other.

"Get to packing. You're coming with me."

PASTOR JONES

CHAPTER 18

❧ I sat on the front porch, swatting flies that circled around my Coca-Cola can sitting on top of my card table. The air was clear, and the sky was filled with small blue streaks that zigzagged into the clouds. I envisioned Big Mama sitting on a visible mass in the sky, looking down with her beautiful wide smile that I remembered.

"What I wouldn't do to have you back, Mama." I sighed, talking to the clouds as if she could hear me.

I shuffled my feet in the fresh mud that accumulated from yesterday's rain. My mind shifted to last night's board meeting. After only five minutes into the meeting, it went left. Having a brand-new building and dealing with animated black folks wasn't a good combination.

———

I slapped my hand down on the table, frustrated by the

cackling that took place amongst the female board members. The men in the room moved their heads back and forth, following their conversations. I was determined to gain order before Mother Gaines bounced her shoulders out of the socket, while clearly enjoying the commentary going back and forth. I wish I had a whip to crack so everyone would quiet down.

"Ladies and gentlemen, why are we arguing over pews? I've created a simple and effective solution. Is anyone listening? What is the problem, doggonit?"

"Say it again so they can hear you, Passuh," Mother Gaines suggested, with her bone straight gray hair stuck to her forehead. It seems as if she was giving her routine wigs a break this week.

"All we have to do is move the pews that were salvaged from the fire. We can position them in a way that will make the sanctuary look full. I know it's a much bigger space than before but taking on another expense isn't a smart move right now."

"Let me see that in writing," Mother Agnes scoffed.

"What is the big deal?" I screamed. "We can only afford minimal décor right now. Our budget is no longer plentiful as years past."

"Oh, now you want to be precautious about overspending, Daddy?" Missy squealed across the table with her rare concession in board meetings.

"Girl, I will slap you into…" I motioned my hands to grab her and then I pulled back, remembering I had witnesses. I was beyond tired of her smart mouth these days. Without Beanie, she no longer had filters and we were constantly getting into it. Diarrhea of the mouth is what I called it. That tongue was moving way too much for my taste. I made a mental note to address her behavior once the meeting was over.

"You've had some overnight metamorphosis going on, gal. Now you are sounding like Olivia."

Her shoulders sagged after being called out in front of the others.

"Please, Daddy."

"Enough," Mother Smithfield growled, shaking her cane to the side. "We're supposed to be civilized Christian folks. What in the world is going on today? Is it a full moon?" Mother's impatient attributes kicked in. She didn't like long meetings, especially with a Bingo tournament going on at the Elks Lodge.

"That's what they say," Deacon Freemon interjected, resting his elbow on the table and putting his fist under his chin.

"Now, Missy, I don't know what's gotten into you with your new-found sassiness, but you better get it together quick. Do you hear me, gal?" Mother Smithfield's stern expression meant to back down, or else the back-hand motion was soon to come to a cheek near you.

She put her head down in shame, scooting low in her seat. "Yes, Ma'am." If no one else could put Missy in check, Mother Smithfield sure could. Missy looked up to her as a grandmother and never once pushed her buttons once her stern expression appeared.

"That's not only your father, but he is also your Overseeing Passuh. So, you better put some respect on his name when spitting words of venom out of that trashy mouth of yours."

Ha, that's what I always say too, Mother. Get her. Put some respect on my name, gal.

I sat back, viewing Missy's sheepish look in disgust. I wanted my sweet daughter back that I remembered from years ago. I didn't know who this woman was sitting before me.

Mother Smithfield looked around the room with a jarring stare. "As for the rest of you buffoons. If Passuh desires to wait before we get more pews in place, so be it. Trying to design and replenish a church is a major undertaking financially. It has already cost us over a million dollars to get the outer structure completed. How is it y'all have it stuck in your head that we got money to burn like that?"

"Shole did. We actually spent a little over a million once you calculate finance charges from the bank," Mother Gaines agreed, tapping her tiny fingers on the table.

She looked back at Mother Gaines with a nod. "Thanks for

reminding me of that, Mother. That is also an important fact."

"Anytime," Mother Gaines gloated.

"Passuh has been a part of a major renovation project before when Earline Jones was alive, so why do you question him now?" Mother Smithfield said with base in her voice.

"I know that's right," Sister Mary said, scribbling every word on her notepad and winking at Deacon Freemon. It wasn't a secret that they were fooling around with one another again. Mary's husband stopped coming to church and it was a mystery if she was even still married to him.

Mother Smithfield continued with everyone at attention. "He's been doing this kind of stuff long before any of you became board members. So, who are you to tell him how to do it now?"

"But Mother, we have members sitting on the side walls in fold-up chairs because there aren't enough seats for everyone," Deacon Freemon interjected with a look of concern.

Mary locked eyes with his and his look of concern vanished as he licked his lips.

"Who cares? These new folks coming in the last few Sundays are just being down right nosey. Newness brings out all kinds of folks. They don't care nothing about getting membership with Mt. Zion. They just want to see what they see and then run and tell how Mt. Zion overcame that fire. Those fold-up chairs won't be lined up for long. Trust me on that," Mother Smithfield answered.

"True," Mother Mary concurred, holding her pen straight up and licking her lips right back at the Deacon.

"Yeah, that's how they do when you become a popular mega church," Mother Gaines said.

"You wait until about a month or so. Y'all won't see any of them folks." Mother Smithfield was right. It was all about television and bright lights for some. Half the people that attended as recent as last Sunday's service had never stepped foot in Mt. Zion until that day.

Mother Gaines nodded her head and grinned at her friend taking charge. "Tell it, sis. Tell it." She swished her shoulders from side to side in agreement.

"Shame before God y'all acting this way over some doggone pews," Mother Smithfield hissed.

"I beg to differ," Mother Agnes said, holding up one finger and sitting up pridefully. "We have the right to voice our opinion and we need new pews! Everything that Pastor Jones decides isn't always right. We have pews that smell like smoke and it's hard to get that smell out of oak wood seats once it's ingrained. Since when do we agree with everything he says? He's been wrong before and isn't that one of the reasons why we kicked him off the board in the past...bad decision making?"

"Hush your mouth." She slammed her fist on the table. "Folks can't never move on with their lives once they've changed. Church folks will always remind you of your sins, even after God has forgiven. So, who asked you?" Mother Smithfield lashed back. She was in the *zone* and it was best to just sit and listen as she demanded full control of the conversation. No one could win an argument with her once she got to the point of no return, no matter how hard they tried.

"Alright, alright, next topic. Lord have mercy," I said with my hand on my forehead. My head was hurting so bad, it felt like it had a heartbeat. "Sister Mary, what's next on the agenda?"

She batted her eyes, looking down at the piece of paper in front of her. She then looked back up and responded, "Prayer rotation."

"Alright. We need to rotate prayer visits between the homeless shelter and the sick and shut-in. Any volunteers?"

Mother Smithfield kept looking over at Mother Agnes as if she was going to snatch out her false teeth and fling them across the table.

The two ladies fell out a few weeks ago about who was supposed to oversee the filling up of the communion cups for first Sunday. It got ugly in the kitchen. All we know is Mother Smithfield splashed grape juice all down Mother Agnes's pretty white suit. Afterwards, Mother Agnes said she forgave her, but I knew that to be a lie. I watched her eyeball Mother Smithfield up and down, while sitting on the other side of the table. I knew both well enough to know their battle wasn't over, it had just begun.

Mother Agnes's wrinkled hands were probably balled up underneath the table, ready for some action. I could feel her pain as there's nothing more horrific than coming to church in your Sunday's best, only to get grape juice splattered all over it. That would deplete every bit of confidence I walked in with if that happened to me. She went from fashionista to a ragamuffin in a split second. I'm sure when she walked away, she had an eternal reminder embedded in her head not to mess with Mother Shirley Smithfield.

Meanwhile, no one raised their hand for prayer rotation duties. "Okay, well, I'll have to start appointing folks since I'm not getting a response."

"How 'bout you appoint yourself for the more difficult cases," Mother Agnes uttered.

"Like who?"

"Why don't you take on the task and pray for that ole devilment, Olivia Wallace." Mother Agnes's suggestion was worse than a prison death sentence. I felt a vibration shoot up my hips as images of Mother Smithfield choking her out flashed through my brain. At that point, I almost wanted my visions to come into fruition.

"So out of order. Oh, you got jokes, Mother?" I asked with sarcasm, thumping my fingers down on the table.

"It's not a joking matter. I'm dead serious. No one wants to deal with her and since you're one of the reasons why she's here, why don't you handle that?"

"I don't have anything to do with why she's here, Mother. My God. You know what they say when you assume, don't you?" I clasped my hands together, trying to remain calm. She had that *I'm feeling froggy* look in her eyes, moving her chapped lips up and down as if she was searching for moisture.

"Well, do it then. Pray for the woman. I'm here every day, monitoring the shelter. I haven't seen you visit not once." She put her index finger up to represent the number one.

"Can I get her, Passuh? Can I just get her...?" Mother Smithfield looked over with disdain, while asking for permission to chime in and initiate more verbal abuse.

I put my hand up. "I got this one, Mother." I pointed over at the note taker. "Mary, put me down to pray for Olivia every Wednesday after noonday prayer, please."

Everyone whispered in unison, "You sure, Pastor?"

"You heard what I said." I grinned mischievously at Mother Agnes. She was one member I'd had to force myself to be nice to over the years and it was obviously not working in my favor at the moment. "Happy, Agnes?"

"That's Mother Agnes to you, sugar." She winked proudly.

I got your sugar.

I shook my head and whispered under my breath, "Lord, have mercy." I learned to pick my battles wisely and I wasn't interested in going down that long road back and forth with a seventy-two-year-old great grandmother.

"Ain't it just like God to have you pray for your enemies?" She smirked.

I mushed my hand into my neck, trying to brace myself and monitor my words. "Alright, meeting adjourned. I can't take no mo'."

PASTOR JONES
CHAPTER 19

I sat outside on my porch, rocking back and forth. It was another hot day in North Carolina. The forecast called for a few showers, but the way the sun beamed down on the sidewalk, I could fry my entire breakfast on the cement in front of me if needed. There was no way rain was coming down on a day like today. Not in all this heat.

I sat back with a half-smile on my face. I became tickled at the thought of Mother Smithfield taking my side in front of others last night. Normally, she was partial, but Mother Agnes always seemed to bring out the worst in her.

Tonya walked out onto the porch, plopping down onto the white matching rocking chair, shifting my thoughts.

"You alright, dear?" I asked, monitoring her body language.

She looked so depressed without Micah.

"I guess. I'm having a hard time accepting that Micah isn't coming back. It's like a bad dream."

"Michelle is doing a fine job taking care of him though.

Think of it that way. He is doing well with his mother."

"Yeah, I know." She sighed.

I was happy for Michelle. She needed a fresh start, along with finding her independence. She had lived off of her family's earnings for so long, it was going to be a struggle joining the workforce. Word on the street was Andrew Hanks decided to stay in Durham with relatives once he returned and did his damage. Knowing that he was out there possibly looking for her was devastating to me. I needed to somehow find him before he found her and the child he created.

"Henry?" Tonya said in a sheepish voice.

"Yes, baby girl?"

"You ready to go inside? It's hot out here." She wiped sweat off her arms.

"Not yet. I'm enjoying the breeze. You should always appreciate the breeze that relieves you from a hot situation. You feel it?"

I didn't hear anything for a few minutes and then she spoke with a whine. "I guess. That sounded like something you would've said in one of your sermons."

I looked over at her again and chuckled. "Habit, I guess."

She looked up with sorrowful eyes and said, "I miss Micah and I want him back."

The gloss in her eyes detected that she wanted me to do

something about the situation, but it just wasn't my place. "Well, like I said before, maybe we can adopt another child. The process is long, but I'm sure it can be done if that's what you really want." I leaned over, putting my arms around her shoulder.

She made another long sigh, turning to me as if a light bulb flashed across her forehead. "I know...Maybe you can talk to Michelle about allowing us to keep him on the weekends? That will allow her to have some time to herself and I can continue to bond with Micah. You think?"

"We'll see." I was skeptical as she was becoming obsessive with getting Micah back in her presence. But, anything would be better than seeing her mope around for weeks at a time. It just wasn't healthy. "Listen, you got to find something else to occupy your time until then, sweetheart. You're going to worry yourself sick about that boy."

She leaned deeper into my chest. "What do you suggest?"

'I rubbed my beard, thinking about last night. I didn't know if she was going to go for being one of the individuals on the prayer roster, but I sure was going to ask.

I cleared my throat. "Why don't you help me at the homeless shelter?"

Her eyes flashed up at me with uncertainty. "Really? You would want me to help you with that?"

"Why not? I mean, that's what most first ladies do anyway, right?"

She laughed. "*No,* that's not what most first ladies do. There isn't a book written about first lady duties, so don't even try it. Plus, I'm not the missionary type anyway."

You really ain't the first lady type either, but...

"How do you know what type you are in the ministry, if you've never tried to help anyone else but yourself?" I played in her hair while she exhaled with a long pause.

Tonya had an excuse for every day of the week. I wish I didn't gravitate towards her so quickly after Sylvia's death. I didn't want to be alone at the time, so I settled for the woman that gave me the most attention. But, once I realized some of her quirky ways, I wanted to run in the other direction. Unfortunately, we'd already tied the knot before I discovered her true colors.

We were married in front of an overflowing congregation that believed in our union. Not even a year into our marriage, I realized she was lazy, self-centered, and selfish in her own right. She made me feel like she was only with me for the prestige and money.

As each year passed, she made our marriage all about her. I called it, "The Tonya Show." If it didn't go her way, it wasn't going to happen. I've spent years trying to help her break these cycles of habits and she has at least tried to make some minimal attempts to change. She woke up and realized one day that it can't be all about her, when I have a congregation full of souls to nurture.

I never once forced her to be part of the church, but I'm sure she knew what she was getting into when she said, "I do" to a generational preacher. The more she lacked ambition, the more cellulite seemed to creep onto those hips. Her yearly body expansion moved faster than Amazon book sales as she sat in a pile of do-nothing day after day, while I ministered around the city of Durham.

"Listen. You gonna have to start getting more involved with the church. You're a great cook, you clean the house well when you get the chance, but now it's time to start acting like a pastor's wife."

I had to cross my fingers while telling that bold-face lie. She ain't cleaned nothing in over three years and her cooking always had me guzzling down water afterwards, to lessen the sting from her over peppery concoctions.

Her eyes jumped as she rocked back and forth, looking as if she was flattered by my sudden false praise.

She patted around her face in an attempt to avoid leaking makeup as it gushed out of her pores and down her neck, due to the hot sun. The heat was melting down her Mary Kay facial masterpiece. She dabbed her cheeks with her fingers, giving a second attempt in keeping her makeup intact.

"I will try and be more supportive, Henry. I promise." Her fingers dropped as she gave a look of protest. Her folded arm formation said something different.

"Good. Your first mission will be to render prayer at the homeless shelter and eventually take ownership of running the daily operations. Right now, we have Mother Agnes in that role and she isn't a good fit for that position. You would be perfect working with some of the women there. They need help with finding clothing for interviews and I can see you now, trying to give everyone in the building a Mary Kay facial."

We both laughed in unison as her spirit lifted. "Okay." She hesitated. "I can do that. Piece of cake."

"Good. Your first case will be *Olivia*."

She moved around in her seat, raising her head off my chest and pressing her nails in her hips. "As in Olivia Wallace, the arsonist?"

I didn't blink. I knew that was coming and I prepared myself by bracing the handles on the rocking chair. "Yes."

"Considering how bad she looked at the Christmas dinner, I doubt if she'll even have that much time left for a prayer."

"Perhaps. Just do the best you can."

"Let me guess. This was your assignment, but you're throwing it on me. Right?" She was very familiar with how I operated when dealing with tough situations.

"Something like that. It's a test for all of us, so please help a brother out."

She laughed loudly, playfully slapping me on the leg, knowing that I was serious as a heart attack. Her arm met mine as she put it around me and said, "Okay, preacher man. I will spare you the misery of doing things you don't want to do. I owe you one anyways for putting up with me and my selfishness after all these years."

You got that right.

She kissed me on the cheek and gazed at the beautiful skyline. I reached down to hold her hand. I was glad that she was finally receptive to my needs and not just hers. *I need a first lady, not just a hand in marriage. From the looks of it, maybe she's ready to finally come back around and be just that.*

NATALIA

CHAPTER 20

I'm gonna bring that creep down to his knees.

God knows I wasn't expecting to hear all of Michelle's truths in one sitting that night during my visit, but I'm glad she trusted me enough to share it. I was passionate about helping women and now determined more than ever in helping my dear friend through yet another life challenge. It burned me up inside, knowing that men could get away with treating women in this matter. But, it was an unfortunate circumstance that many generations of women faced without any support or mercy from other family members. I paid for Michelle and Micah to stay at the DoubleTree Hotel off Meridian Parkway as long as they needed to be there. I wasn't about to let them be eaten by rats in that filthy halfway house.

"Babe, you okay?"

I blinked into focus, dangling my glass of wine in the air. My blue nail tips grabbed the glass tighter as my thoughts were filled with revenge. Frank chose one of the best sushi joints in

Durham for dinner, of off Hwy 54. He had good taste in dining, along with everything else.

"I'm okay." I sipped slowly.

"What's on your mind, honey bun?" His smile was contagious as I smiled back.

"Do you have any criminal attorney friends I can call? I'm asking for a friend."

He reserved his judgment and responded, "Sure. I have a long list of folks."

He reached his hand over, touching my forearm.

I shivered.

He had my nose wide open…still.

❱ I gave a grin, trying to ease his concern. "I'll be okay, honey. Once I find an attorney to talk to, everything will fall in place."

"Let me guess, it's either to help Michelle or Missy. Right?"

I put the glass down and picked it back up again with nervousness. "Maybe."

His look turned from concern to conspicuous. "You would've made a great activist in the seventies during the women's movement, you know that, right?"

"And you know this, man." I pumped my fist up and reached over and gave him a high five.

#Wakandaforever

"How's your sushi?"

"It's delicious." I shoved a piece of ginger and a section of my California roll into my mouth.

"Yeah, I love this place. It's always good food and positive vibes."

He chugged his can of *Not your father's root beer* down his throat. "Nat, we need to plan our wedding soon." He had dreamy eyes while using his chopsticks to dip his sushi in soy sauce.

"Wedding? No need for that now. We've already did what we had to do to make this thing official."

"But, you deserve to have one. Remember when I told you that you would be the most beautiful bride in Durham?"

I blushed, swirling salad around in ginger dressing. "Yes, I remember that."

"Wouldn't you want the opportunity to have the wedding of a lifetime? Every woman wants a wedding, right? The sky is the limit."

"*Really?*" His company was doing well this year and he now had over twenty employees working for him, so asking was just facetious formality. I knew cost wasn't an issue.

"Yes, really."

"Okay." We touched each other's hand and agreed.

He responded with a big exhale. "Besides, I want my family

to be part of our special day. Henderson is just a hop, skip, and a jump down the highway, so the entire Thomas clan would definitely be in attendance."

"Please don't have your sisters frying chicken for the reception. The entire wedding party will be asleep after chomping down on all that grease."

He laughed loudly, making the couple beside us look over.

"Not to worry, sweet lady. I already have a caterer in mind."

"Let me guess, Bull City Pitmasters?" Our eyes met in agreement.

"You know it. A wedding it is."

I envisioned wearing high heels and waltzing down an aisle in a cream-colored wedding dress. My arms would be covered with lace as my pearl tiara would sit high on my natural curly bun.

"I love you, Nat."

I go into a trance every time he says that.

"Let's go make a baby tonight."

I mashed another piece of sushi in my mouth, choking off the statement and washing it down with the last drop of my sangria. "Having a popped belly in my tight-fitting wedding dress won't work for me. But, I'd love to participate in the acts of making one though."

We belched out laughter together. We could see the other couple laughing too as they were now listening to our conversation.

"Now that's what I'm talking about, sweet lips." He raised his hand high in the air and said, "Waiter...check, please."

MISSY

CHAPTER 21

▸I continued my weekly sessions, waiting for a guest appearance from Beanie. I hoped he would take Dr. Brown's advice and take a break, but then come back to me. I started to miss him in a funny kind of way. I didn't miss his blunt comments, or his high standards, I missed his smile. The smile that warmed my heart and turned my rainy days into sunshine. Of course, he had more to offer than just a smile, but the loss of that resonated the most. I guess I really didn't love him as I had thought. I pondered on what else stood out about him and my mind went blank.

I just hoped wherever he laid his head, he was safe. But, I couldn't continue to rack my brain about his whereabouts. I called him every now and again to check on him, but I never got an answer or a call back. With the engineering firm bogging me down with new projects, it was easy to put him in the back of my brain and not to think about him. Keeping him out of my thoughts and concentrating on spiritual growth was always best. Finding someone in the future when I was ready to date again wasn't going to be tough. I was positive about that, because I now had new standards and qualifications for a mate.

I sat hunched over, struggling to complete my work. I had a pile of papers on each side of my desk. My deadline was to finish all of them by the end of the month. There was no way it was all going to get done in time.

My cell phone buzzed in my pocket, displaying a blocked caller across the screen. Each time, I would look down and then let it go into voicemail. That didn't stop the buzz as it started again every few seconds. I answered, feeling annoyed.

Who could be blowing me up like this?

"Hello?"

"Hello, Pastor Missy."

"Yes?"

"Greetings. My name is Sasha and I'm the woman that Beanie comes home too." She giggled loudly at her own statement.

"Excuse me?" I squinted down at the phone as if I could see who it was talking to me on the other end.

"You didn't hear me, Miss Thang? Shake the wax out of your ears, *chick*. Beanie moved in with me last week. So, with that being said, you can stop wearing that sparkling diamond ring he gave you. I notice you fling it right in front of the cameras, while you call yourself preaching so hard up in the pulpit. No more Beanie Anderson for you, my dear."

"What's your name again?"

"I'm one of your member's sister's friend. I've been attending Mt. Zion for years."

"Why are you calling me? If he's your man, why do I need to know?"

"I just wanted to give you a fair warning, so you can take the opportunity in cashing that rock in. Make a little money while you can, honey. I'm all about sisterhood and I'm just one sister, trying to help another gain some extra cash. Five carats will get you a pretty good down payment for a car or something, don't you think?"

He told her the number of carats I have in my ring? My face glistened with steam.

"I see you're not brave enough to approach me at the church, huh? You're going out the coward way by calling."

"For what? I have him now, homey. But, just in case you want to look at your last Sunday service on video, I sit on the third row right behind him every Sunday. Short Halle Berry haircut, slim waist, cute face. You can't miss me, boo."

No, she didn't. "Well, good for you, Halle Berry wannabe."

"Your ex-man like it."

"Whatever."

"I just wanted to extend a whole-hearted thanks for

messing up a good thing. He's a keeper."

I checked the phone again, but this time viewing with looming sadness. Some nerve she had calling me and some nerve he had, sharing our personal business with a stranger.

"Enjoy my leftovers, fake Halle."

"No problem, sweetness. Oh, forgot to add, I'll put some extra cash in the offering basket this Sunday, so you can get your hair done too. Lately, you've been looking a hot mess." She laughed like a cackling hen being chased in a barn by its owner.

She was quick on her feet and had a comeback for everything I said. "You..." I couldn't find the right words to say.

"Just call me Ms. Anderson."

"Listen you little ..."

"Now, now, Ms. Pastor Girl. Don't worry, since we're both still members, we might need you to officiate the wedding. I'll send you an invite. Is your address..."

I clicked the red button on the screen, ending the call. A flurry of sinister thoughts clouded my vision. I was beyond livid. Words couldn't describe how I felt. I jumped up and started pacing the floor. Bad thoughts surfaced on how I could go against the grain of being a Pastor and find that *garden tool*.

Not Beanie. Not my Beanie.

I glanced at my engagement ring, snatching it off my finger

with force. It felt like I ripped some skin as my legs started to give out, buckling at the thought of it all. Then, I squeezed it back on my finger, not wanting to let go of the idea of someone once wanting to marry me. I had a good mind to pull the video just to see her face. But, at the end of the day, it wouldn't change things…he was her man *now*.

PART IV

EVERYTHING WILL BE ALRIGHT.

"For my thoughts are not your thoughts, neither are your ways my ways," declares the Lord.

Isaiah 55:8

PASTOR JONES

CHAPTER 22

Two weeks later...

❡Everything seemed to fall in place.

The church building was complete inside and out, attracting a diverse set of new members. We were back to having a high time in the Lord and individuals drove across the state of North Carolina to attend our services.

The board lost their fight against my plethora of wisdom. They realized they couldn't win when it came to running and organizing the church. Big Mama Jones handled all church affairs solo before a board ever existed. I was determined to keep some of the same values to reshape the ministry. Eventually, they fell back in love with my ideas and trusting my judgment, now that all the funds borrowed were returned.

Natalia and Frank were planning a glamorous wedding to be held at Mt. Zion within the next few weeks. Mt. Zion had the space that Ebenezer Light House did not, so it was fitting to have their grandiose wedding at Natalia's home church. After creating a guest list, they were already up to over five hundred people. From taste tests, viewing of reception space, and meet and greets with each side of the family, the wedding was going to be a wonderful occasion.

Michelle spent most of her time between rehab, looking for a job, and enjoying every free moment with her child, who was now running and talking up a storm. Her confidence soared, and she was back to looking healthy and fit like she used to. My prayers had been answered.

Beanie never returned to Missy's apartment, nor Mt. Zion for that matter. His absence forced a spiritual shakedown within Missy's soul as she gradually started to change back into the caring pastor, sister, and daughter that everyone once loved. Shortly after she renewed her relationship with God, she announced on a live broadcast that she would be taking a hiatus from pastoral duties and would only minister part-time. It was the best decision she could've made to finally get herself together and heal from Tommy's death. I admired her strength and happily jumped right back into the spotlight to take her place.

Tonya had a new-found happiness and because of that, things were getting better between us. Her wish to keep Micah every weekend came true. The more he came around, the more the sun shined deep in her heart. He lifted her spirits on a rainy day and made her feel needed. Better yet, he made her feel *loved*. She had stepped up her game. Not only did she assist with the homeless shelter daily, but she also took full responsibility to run it. Mother Smithfield would help from time to time because the shelter stayed in demand, but the majority of the time, Tonya got the job done solo. She was back to being what I needed her to be, my *First Lady*.

As for me, the rumors faded, and I was all about saving souls these days. I no longer entertained church hiccups and I was all about my *Father's* business. I was doing what Big Mama said I would do and I didn't look back. It was a new day, a new season, and a new praise for God's goodness and mercy that he showered upon all of us.

Everything was perfect until *today*.

———

It was a usual Saturday. Football, Kool-Aid, and finger food. While watching college football, I slouched down in my recliner, smacking my lips to the crunch of popcorn. Tonya emerged through the front door with an indignant glare.

"Henry, oh my God. Henry, you won't believe this one!"

She stood in the doorway, cutting her eyes and breathing heavily.

I cuffed a handful of popcorn and stuffed it in my mouth. My head jerked around. "What is it?"

"Henry, I saw the strangest thing at the shelter today..."

I was agitated as she stood directly in front of the television. She was not following the football code of ethics especially with Alabama and Auburn playing. There were only minutes left in the rival game and I needed her to move out the way ASAP.

"Somebody get shot or something?"

"*No*," she huffed, holding her chest and exhaling with short breaths.

I gave her a side eye as she continued to stand looking confused while puncturing my concentration. "Well, it isn't important then. The game is on, woman. Move out the way, doggone it."

She huffed even harder, taking a few steps to the side and trying to get my full attention.

I stopped chewing for a moment, feeling guilty that I wasn't showing any level of concern. But after all, what could be more important than football? "You come flying up in here like a bat out of hell. Why you are breathing so hard?" I shoved another handful of popcorn into my mouth, exuberating the grand smell of melted butter close to my nostril.

"Henry, I hate to be the carrier of bad news, but Olivia won't be leaving this world anytime soon."

A lump of popcorn caught in my throat. "What do you mean?"

She moved closer to the side of the recliner, gripping my free hand. "I just witnessed her *dancing*."

I just know she didn't say what I think she just said. I plopped the popcorn bag in between my legs, pushing the reclining foot rest to the floor.

"Nah, that ain't possible. The woman can barely walk these days. Missy's been pushing her around in that wheelchair of hers for months."

Tonya gripped my other hand, smearing the butter onto hers and giving a googly-eyed glare. "I know what I saw in the shelter, Henry. I hate to say it, but I think her illness is all an act."

Snatching my hand back and shaking my index finger back and forth with disbelief, I croaked, "Pleezzee tell me you are lying. Nah-uh. No way."

She stepped back, dropping her hand bag off her shoulder and onto the floor. "Who can make stuff like this up, Henry? I walked into the shelter today for a surprise room check. I don't normally go there on Saturdays, but something told me to stop by. And there she was, standing near the window dancing around kicking her legs in and out, side to side. She looked as if she was practicing for a *Cupid Shuffle* contest."

This was some kind of bad. Tonya wasn't known to be a liar, but I couldn't even imagine Olivia being able to do anything after the last time I laid eyes on her. Who would spend all this time, putting on an act that would ruin the chances of ever having her daughter's trust again?

I grunted, still in amazement. "How is that even possible?"

Tonya pushed her fingertips into her hips. "Henry!"

I wriggled to the edge of my seat with my elbow propped on my leg, spilling popcorn onto the rug in front of me.

Tonya protested, "I saw her plain as day. She was listening to an old MC Hammer song and right when it got to the bridge of 'Too Legit to Quit,' she started pop locking and prancing like it was nobody's business."

I guess she loves listening to MC Hammer, huh?

"Pop locking? I wish I could pop her back to California. Ole wench…never mind." The cursing demon jumped on my back. I had several words that came to mind, but just couldn't say them like I wanted to now that I'd been redeemed by the Blood of the Lamb.

Tonya's eyebrows caved in. She knew if I'd gotten to the point of name calling that I was beyond livid.

"And her moves were on point too. That skinny little woman can dance."

I rubbed the sweat off my nose. "No one can have that

kind of precision and balance with a catheter dangling from their privates, Tonya. That's impossible."

How could this be?

"Well, she did, Henry. That catheter was laying on top of the bed with the cord wrapped around it. It's all part of the act."

I leaped out of the chair still holding onto her hands. "That little…come hell or high water, we got to get her out of that shelter. I'm sure she's been plotting on all of us since day one."

Tonya's face balled up with agony. Now that Tonya was Team Jones through and through, she looked deeply into my eyes as if she could feel my pain.

"The sad part is, she didn't even notice me coming or going. The music was blasting, and she was really into it."

"I still don't get it, Tonya. Deacon Freemon carried her in the church just last Sunday. She was pale like a white woman without a touch of sun and her skin was peeling like a snake."

"A *snake?* Yeah, that is a very good description of her right about now."

I rolled my eyes, moving them from the television to hers. "Lord."

She dropped my hands, folding her arms like she always did when she became fed up with my reaction. "Um-hum. Well, she did."

I paused, staring at the television screen and soaking in this unbelievable story. Visions of Missy and Olivia holding hands flashed from that very first time I visited the shelter. How could she be so trifling towards her own flesh and blood?

"This is the last straw. I'm about to take full control of this situation, no matter how Missy feels about her." I rubbed my temple. Olivia's cynicism was really going to hurt Missy after receiving her with open arms.

"What are we going to do to stop her this time?"

With a nervous twitch, I answered, "I have no idea, honey."

"Do you think she'll try to burn the church down again?"

I scrunched my face, not wanting to think about it, especially during the last two plays of the football game. "Nah, if she went to this extent to fool all of us, she has a bigger and better plan in mind. I'm sure she was very methodical and has this one well thought out."

"You might wanna call Missy and warn her."

I rubbed my chin, tugging my beard. "Yeah, I guess you're right."

Another setback. Ain't nobody got time for this!

I shook my head back and forth, inspecting the room for my cell phone. I didn't know how I was going to break the news to Missy.

Tonya quipped with a smug look as she cupped her elbows tighter, "Oh, wait…I just remembered. It might be too late to catch up with her, Henry."

I doubled back with wonder. "What do you mean too late? Too late for what?"

"You don't remember? The seniors are going on their annual trip to Washington D.C. today. They were loading up the van when I left the church."

My heart raced faster than a rocket shooting up in the sky. "Say what?"

I panicked, rubbing my arms while pacing the entire floor. "Why didn't you stop her? Or why didn't you call me, *so I* could've stopped her!"

Cheers permeated through the surround sound speakers connected to the television. I glared over and in large bold letters the results flashed across the sixty-inch screen. Alabama beats Auburn, *again*.

ʾI had to miss out on doing my little football dance this time around. My team bum rushed center field, while my daughter was probably somewhere in the midst of running for her life. I was stressed with worry slithering down my neck. I strived to think straight because the *Roll Tide* chanting was distracting.

I turned back to Tonya with a low mumble of disappointment. "Baby, you should've called me right after you witnessed all of this."

Tonya's eyelids drooped with guilt. "I...I...I wasn't

thinking, Henry. Oh, my goodness, I'm so sorry. I was so shocked by it all that I rushed to get home to tell you about it. It didn't dawn on me until I pulled in the driveway."

"Do you know where they're going while in D.C.?"

She had an inquisitive look. "I guess you don't listen to Sunday morning announcements anymore, huh? They are going to the National Museum of African American History for the weekend."

I slapped my hand across my forehead. "Ugh. Yeah, that's right. I forgot all about that."

I scattered around the room, still in search of my cell phone. I pushed my hand down inside the recliner cushion, pulling the black covered case out of its hiding place.

I quickly dialed Missy's number.

Tonya stood in front of me, smoothing her hands over her face in frustration. This was the worst. Not knowing what Olivia was up to boggled my mind.

While I waited for an answer, I turned to Tonya and asked, "Is Natalia and Michelle going on this trip too?"

"Only Natalia. Frank is driving the church van and Missy is chaperoning Olivia, Smithfield, and Gaines in a rental."

Fix it, Jesus.

Admittedly, I became scared. Fear wasn't supposed to be upon me, but it crept its way all down my spine. I sat back in the recliner with the phone close to my ear. Each time my hands landed on the redial button, I felt myself emotionally shrinking. I was sick and tired of Satan playing games with me and my family.

Answer, gal.

Enough is enough, devil. Get thee behind me.

I started thinking out loud, "If that woman lays even a fingertip on my child, I will…"

Tonya leaned over, rubbing my shoulders. "Henry, it's going to be okay. God will always take care of his own. Let's drive up there to make sure Missy is safe. How does that sound?"

I hesitated, but Tonya was right. God was going to come through, I knew that, but my faith suddenly withered. I had to get to my daughter and handle this demon once and for all. All of this didn't make sense, but God's strength was attainable to end Olivia's long string of charades.

With heavy eyes and a heavy heart, I stomped into the bedroom without a response. I threw the iPhone X down and pulled a suitcase from underneath the bed. It was time to take a trip. Tonya and I bumped hips, throwing outfits in the large Louis Vuitton suitcase. The memories of Olivia's last acts etched inside my head as the Holy Spirit twitched at my ear.

Missy is in danger.

MISSY

CHAPTER 23

It was a beautiful warm day. The weatherman announced on the radio a slight chance of fog and precipitation towards the end of the day. However, the clouds were clear as I drove bumper to bumper down Highway 95 North. The traffic was thick leaving out of Richmond, VA. Flashing lights blinked on the side of the road, warning drivers to move with caution. Apparently, a nasty three-car pile-up occurred in the third lane.

Everyone seemed content in the spacious SUV I rented from Alamo Rentals. While Mother Gaines stared out the window, viewing everything on her side, Mother Smithfield was yapping nonstop and telling her usual war stories of growing up in Durham. Every few minutes, Mother Gaines laughed at her corny jokes and put her hands over her mouth as if she was listening to something profound. But after an hour into the ride, the laughter faded. Meanwhile, Olivia laid across the front seat fast asleep, with her stringy long hair hung to one side and her hands clasped to the other.

❦I wanted to make this trip a memorable one. So, instead of riding with the other seniors in the church van, I thought it would be more intimate to drive with my three-favorite people in a separate car. Frank and Natalia tailed behind us in the van. It had over two hundred thousand miles, but the twelve-seater Toyota purred like a kitten. I glanced through the rear view every few minutes to ensure they were not far behind me.

Along with my crew, there were four church mothers and three deacons tagging along for this joyous occasion. They were ecstatic about such an opportunity. We were going; rain, sleet, snow or shine. Nothing was going to stop us from viewing all the rich African American history the museum had to offer.

Four hours into the ride, Mother Smithfield realized that she was only being heard by the highway gods. Mother Gaines nodded every now and again, but it was time to turn up the music, which would politely give her a hint to hush. I turned the volume up a notch after seeing the name *The Walls Group* appearing on the playlist. I hadn't sung in a while. But, I had an urge to loosen my vocals as I mouthed along to "Mighty You Are." My notes synced right in with theirs.

"They can sing, can't they?" Mother Smithfield interjected.

"Yes, Ma'am, they can. You like them?"

"Oh, yes, they harmonize well."

"They're one of my favorite groups. Maybe I can get them

to come for one of our youth revivals."

"You can do that, gal? The children would love that, I'm sure."

I looked back in the rear-view mirror. Mother Smithfield squirmed around every few seconds, seeming uncomfortable.

"You alright, Shirley?" Mother Gaines asked, noticing her extensive state of the wiggles.

"Chile, just these swollen feet of mine, that's all."

"Well, do you have on your special shoes?'

"Nah, chile. These ole toes needed some air, that's probably why they hurtin', huh?"

"I suppose *so*."

Before the song ended, the two ladies perked up, sparking another frivolous conversation. Laughing and joking was their usual pastime when they shared moments alone. It was only when others were watching that they showed off by throwing verbal jabs at one another. They met each other in the sandbox way back when and have been *frick and frack* ever since. Before I knew it, their voices escalated above the music.

"Shirley Smithfield, you know you gotta cut a whole chicken into eight parts when you buy it like that. Come on now. Don't play crazy."

"If I want to cut it down the middle and leave it like that, I can. There isn't a law book on how to cut chicken, Odessa!"

"That's the dumbest thing I've ever heard. So, you just gonna leave the dark and the white hooked together?"

"Doggone right. Just the way I like it."

They burst into laughter.

Mother Gaines blurted, "You ain't a real woman if you don't know how to cut a whole chicken, Shirley."

"Lies. My children ate it however I fixed it. I've even cooked it for the church like that once."

"Shame on you, woman." Mother Gaines chuckled.

"Ain't no shame in my game, honey. A chicken is a chicken, no matter how you slice it."

Mother Gaines's old-time country girl philosophy surely wasn't one of mine. I had no clue on how to cut a chicken into its proper parts and truth be told, I wasn't trying to learn.

"Shirley, I bet you would mess up oatmeal if it didn't come with instructions."

"Chile, I cook with love. I don't follow instructions on no doggone box. That's blasphemy, coming from a country woman."

They started laughing again as I smiled through the rear-view mirror. I looked over at Olivia. After all the loud laughter, I didn't understand how she slept so peacefully. She resembled a heavenly angel stretched across the seat and I was so proud to have my biological *mama* sitting right beside me.

"You alright over there, Olivia?" I nudged her arm, hoping to get a positive response.

"I'm doing just fine, sweet daughter." She cocked her head up, smiling at me and then put it back down.

Minutes later, we passed the sign I had been waiting to view. It read: *Welcome to Maryland, The Free State.*

MISSY

CHAPTER 24

❧ I pulled up into the Embassy Suites hotel parking lot, anxiously awaiting to free my legs. Being in the same position for so long had me a little numb and I needed to stretch. Mother Smithfield swung the heavy metal door open on her side and jumped out onto the cement. She was barefoot, throwing her orthopedic shoes in front of her. I trotted to the back of the jeep for Olivia's wheelchair. With both hands, I helped her out of the vehicle and into the chair. She sat back as I adjusted her leg rest. She plopped her legs on top of the two metal foot frames as soon as they were snapped in tightly.

Mother Gaines exited the vehicle, making a small hop. For a sixty-seven-year-old woman, she was in fantastic shape. I had never seen her sick or needing assistance from anyone. We nicknamed her the "Holy Ghost Runner" because even at her age, she was still running up and down the aisle, praising God with speed.

As we all headed towards the hotel sidewalk, the van pulled up, letting out all passengers. We waited so that we could walk in together. While pushing Olivia through the glass sliding doors, she tilted her head up and said, "Today is going to be a good day, my dear."

"You think so?"

"I know so, sweetheart."

I shrugged my shoulders. I hadn't seen her this happy in months.

"Can we grab a small bite to eat after we check in? I've somehow gained an appetite." She sat up at attention.

"Sure. What do you have a taste for?"

"Wherever you want to take me, love."

A devilish grin was plastered across her face. It threw me for a loop. I hadn't seen that facial expression since her first appearance at Mt. Zion, when we showed up in the church parking lot a few years back.

"You okay?" I asked.

"Oh, yeah. I'm feeling grand, my child."

Minutes later, we were loaded back in the car and getting ready to head down Highway 395 in search of a fine dining establishment. I glared at my cell phone before starting the engine.

Seven missed calls?

I looked over at Olivia. "This looks important. Give me a second to call Daddy back," I said, holding up one finger.

Olivia's voice rose. "He can wait. You've been catering to him all your life, it's Mommy's time now."

Her eyes twitched with her lips turned to the side.

I ignored her hateful demeanor and responded politely, "Either you're very hungry or very tired. I will call him once we get to the restaurant. Cool?" I giggled at her silent cry for attention, tipping my phone into the cup holder beside me.

"Good, now let's roll," she said, snapping her fingers as if she was the Queen of Sheba and I was her lowly servant.

I leaned down to adjust my seat, connecting the GPS. I was in the mood for fried chicken and vegetables. The GPS scanned the area for the nearest country-style food joint. There was location less than eight miles away.

"I found something. Now, we can roll." I put the car in gear and merged onto Highway 395.

———————

My phone buzzed nonstop in the cup holder, notifying me of text messages. I picked the phone up to view while holding the steering wheel steady.

DaddyJones: Missy call me ASAP. Olivia is the devil. She's a fake, a fraud, an imposter! Get far away from her as you can, gal. NOW.

Another text chimed in:

DaddyJones: I'm on my way, daughter. Call 911!!!!

I looked away, bringing a gaze to the center of Olivia's eyes, which resembled mine. She twitched with a smug familiar look. Her eyes signaled *trouble*.

I didn't want to show alarm, but when I looked with my peripheral, she planted a silver revolver onto the right side of my dome.

"Issssss thatttt a gun?" Mother Gaines leaned forward, shouting in panic, and bouncing her shoulders up and down.

"It sure is, Mother dear." Without hesitation, Olivia reached back and hit her in the center of her forehead. A long howling scream emerged as she slumped to the side.

Mother Smithfield leaned forward with a manic roar. "Are you crazy?"

"If that's what you want to call it." Olivia winced.

"You are truly a mad woman, you know that? I told you she wasn't right in the head, Missy. I told y'all this tramp was up to no good."

Olivia ignored the commentary, thumping the gun against my shoulder with a harsh command. "Drive."

I eyeballed over in disgust. "And to think, I really believed you this time. What do you want from me now, you fake cancer patient?"

"Wise up, my dear. What I've always wanted from you and your sorry behind daddy—my freaking *money*!" She grit her teeth, pushing words through the open gaps in her mouth.

I was hot like fish grease and couldn't concentrate any longer, swerving in and out of traffic.

Olivia turned to the back, leaning towards Mother Smithfield. "Pull out that Gold Platinum card I've seen you use for church purchases. I'm sure the sky is the limit on that line of credit you got there. I bet I can get my money and then some." She smirked.

Mother Smithfield ignored her plea, looking into the rear-view mirror at me.

Olivia pressed the trigger, making it click. "Did you hear what I said, Ms. Shirley? If you don't, I'm blasting Miss Goodie Two Shoes' brains out."

I looked back at Mother Smithfield. She wasn't moved nor disturbed by Olivia's threats. She shuffled through her bag while trying to mouth a message, but I wasn't good at reading lips. My anxiety roared, and I could barely keep the car in between the white lines of the highway.

Olivia continued to wiggle her gun around. The next thing I knew, the metal piece hit me across my face, knocking my head alongside the window. I put my hand over the newly dented spot in my head and wailed, "Why are you so evil?"

"Y'all Negroes must think I'm stupid. I see the eye game you got going on. Drive and get me something to eat before I really show you how evil I can get!"

Mother Smithfield took the card out of her purse and dangled it high in the air. "If I give it to you, will you leave us be?"

Without an answer, Olivia reached back for the card, grabbed it, then reached down and hit Mother across her swollen feet. Blood gushed upward, squirting across the top of the vehicle.

Mother endured the pain, pushing forward and striking back. She grabbed Olivia's hair and balled it up around her big knuckles. "Jesus will protect this car. Yes, he will. Nobody but you, Father, can REBUKE IT."

Olivia held the card in one hand, pushing Mother Smithfield off with the other.

I reached over, getting a jab or two in, while still trying to control the car. I was striking for every missed birthday, every missed holiday and every lie she ever told me. I despised her at this point and I wanted her life to end immediately. I had never been so mad at someone in my life and every fiber in my being wanted Ms. Olivia Wallace to disappear for good.

*Within seconds, a weird ripping could be heard. She yelled at the top of her lungs, "Ouch!"

Mother Smithfield yanked a handful of curly strands from Olivia's head and waved it in the air with pride like an African flag.

"What the…my *hair*!" Olivia screamed as if she was Sampson from the Bible losing her strength.

Her eyes magnified as she waved over the missing hair area with her long fingers. She stuffed the credit card in her bra with the quickness. The gun she tucked away inside her coat pocket. It didn't matter if she had calmed down, I continued to let out my frustration across her bony face.

"Missy, stop. I don't want to hurt you. Stop."

The passenger side door swung open as the pressure of her body weight pressed against the latch. She was stifled by my blows, trying desperately to hold onto anything she could get her hands on. I prayed that I could eject her body onto the highway and an eighteen-wheeler could finish the job. But, that didn't happen as she held on tightly.

"Slow down. Please, Missy, slow down."

I swerved back and forth, trying to gain composure. But, it was too late. My anxiety went left, and I couldn't reel my emotions back in. "For what? I'm tired of you hurting me. Now, it's time to hurt you."

She pulled out the gun and fired towards the wooded area on the side of the highway. "Do as I said, little girl, before I kill everyone in this car."

Her wish was my command. I pushed my feet on the metal, swerving onto the emergency lane and landing slap smack-dab into a murky area full of trees and mud on the side of the highway. Olivia jumped out and dived onto the ground. The car was still moving as I now tried to gain control. I was unsettled, peering through the rear-view mirror to check on the ladies in the back.

"Mother? Are you okay?" I reached back as the car bounced deeper into the woods. When I moved both hands front and center to steer the car, a sudden jolt bulldozed my head onto the dashboard. It was apparent I had run into something big, clunky, and out of place. Something that had enough force to implode air bags on both sides.

I gasped for air from the chalky substances released.

What was it? Where am I? Where's Olivia?

A tree. I hit a tree?

The car was coiled around a tree. Glass splattered across the front seat. I pulled my head up slowly as everything was blurred. I laid my head back down on the dashboard, zooming in and out of consciousness. My strength was gone.

Father God, help us.

MISSY

CHAPTER 25

⬧ Chemicals of the air bag saturated throughout as the truck tilted to the side. I was coherent enough to notice blood dripping from my fingertips. Glass stuck to my skin, my head, and my face. Across my arms…blood. The feeling in my leg was desensitized. I was slumped over, feeling helpless.

Suddenly, I heard a voice through the cracked window. "Ma'am, can you hear me? Can you hear me?"

It was a Hispanic-looking officer, wearing a Maryland police badge and hat, with a beam of terror across his face. The light from his flashlight bounded around the inside of the SUV.

How are the others? Are they alive? Save us, Jesus.

Soon after the doors swung open with several uniformed men surrounding us, masks of oxygen were clamped onto my face. I could hear one of the men say, "Make sure you've got all three of them. We might need the Jaws of Life to remove the driver."

Jaws of Life?

My body was embedded into the dashboard. I couldn't feel a thing. I didn't know how many seconds, minutes, or hours had passed since the initial impact. But, I felt cold and disoriented. I whispered to the paramedic standing in front of me, "Are they okay? Are my passengers okay? Mother Gaines? Mother Smithfield, can you hear me?"

"Shhhhh, don't worry yourself. We will take good care of them. You're going into shock. Stay still. We're here for you." There was a long pause. As voices lingered in and out, I could only hear the workers. I couldn't hear Mother Smithfield or Mother Gaines' voices. I was cold. So very cold.

"Oh, my God, that's Missy Jones!" a person in uniform hovering over me yelled.

"No, the heck it ain't," someone responded back.

"Yes, it is. I know that face anywhere. I watch her every Sunday on cable."

"You don't say." He paused as if he was taking another look. "Sure is her."

My body continued to tremor. Tingling shots of friction pulsed through my entire body.

Before I knew it, the rings on my hands were being stripped off with a set of pliers. "This may hurt a little, Ma'am, but we have to get them off. They're cutting off your circulation since your hands are swollen."

I nodded.

I could hear metal clanking against metal as each ring popped off, making tinkering noises against the dashboard.

My pretty rings Beanie bought me. They're gone.

❧ I shut my eyes again…the voices were becoming faint. For some reason, I thought I heard the word, "Clear!"

I blinked and then it went *black*.

NATALIA

CHAPTER 26

Every senior that attended the trip piled up in the waiting room at John Hopkins Hospital. We had no information on the status of our loved ones. We waited patiently for a doctor to appear with some form of news.

For some reason, I felt strange. A remorseful spirit lingered in the room.

I turned to Frank and said, "I think we lost someone."

"Don't say that. They will all get through this like they always do."

"But, what if they don't?" I put my hands over my mouth, thinking about it.

He took a deep breath and said, "I sure hope not. I sure hope this is one time your instincts are wrong."

"What do you think happened to Olivia?"

He sighed. "I don't know, but you were spot-on with that one. She spent a lot of time sweet talking Missy. I can't believe she didn't feel anything for her after all the time they've spent together."

"Poor girl. She really loved that woman."

Frank crossed his legs and pulled me towards him. "As my mama used to say, a leopard doesn't change its spots."

He viewed the pain in my eyes.

My heart ached. "You know what all of this is?"

He looked over. "What, sweetie?"

"God's distraction. He had to do something so big, so that we would have no choice but to turn to him."

He sighed as his eyes traveled around the room. "I believe that wholeheartedly, Nat. It's going to be hard for folks to come back from all of this. If this all has a spiritual meaning, we better take heed."

"You got that right. But, I believe we'll come out even stronger than ever before."

"Amen, sweet lips. Amen."

Mother Agnes inched over to the edge of her seat, sitting across from us. "When will they let us know something?"

I shrugged my shoulders, blowing her off. My mind was wandering left and right, and I felt so bad about the entire situation. I bent my head down in prayer. If someone was dead, I prayed for comfort for the others. But, just in case all remained amongst the living, I prayed for healing.

A long period of time lapsed before we finally got word on what was going on. Pastor Jones and First Lady came rushing through the double doors of the plain décor waiting area, just in time to hear the updates. An Asian doctor, standing about five feet three appeared, wearing a long white coat that touched the middle of his knees. He entered the room with a serious face, looking eager to make us privy of the status.

"Members of the Jones, Smithfield, and Gaines families?" he inquired.

Pastor caught his breath and raised his hand. "Yes."

"Can I speak to you in the back, please?"

He glanced over at me. "I need my other children to come with me. Come on, Nat and Frank."

We followed the doctor to a secluded office area. There were only business offices down this long hallway on the first floor of the hospital.

"Are they okay?" I queried.

"The young girl named Missy should be coming out of surgery any moment now. She's in bad shape."

"Bad shape how?" Pastor screeched.

She has a broken hip and two cracked femurs. But, the good news is she'll live. She's young and healthy, so we expect her to bounce back from this."

I gripped Pastor's arm, waiting for the rest. "Okay…"

"As for the two older women…Ms. Shirley Smithfield…"

"Yes?" Pastor said, fully alert.

"She's actually doing better than expected. A few cuts and bruises, but other than that, she can be moved to a regular room sometime tonight. A true miracle, that lady."

I blew my breath. "Whew." I knew if Mother Smithfield made it, then Mother Gaines was somewhere sitting up full of energy, ready to race down the hospital stairs.

The doctor's facial expression changed with his next few sentences. "Unfortunately, we were unable to save Odessa Gaines. She died at the scene."

"What?" Pastor's lips thinned. His skin became flushed with a weak chai tea coloration. He stumbled and sniffed as if a heavy weight settled on his heart. "Repeat that again, sir," he said with a lower tone.

"I'm sorry Mr. Jones, but Odessa Gaines was DOA at the scene of the accident. It looks like she took a hard blow to the head and there was nothing we could do to save her. Her brain hemorrhaged from the blow."

I crumbled inside, and my heart plunged in despair. Not only did I feel pain for Pastor Jones, but also for Mother Smithfield. They fought often like two little school girls, but they were thick as thieves.

Pastor bent over in pain. The doctor reached down, patting his back. "I know it's a lot to absorb. Take your time. It's okay."

"Can we see them?" I asked with hope disintegrating from my voice.

"It will be awhile, but yes, you can see all of them probably in the morning."

Mother Gaines, the most vibrant and well put together member of the church, had gone home to be with the Lord. The *Holy Ghost Runner* was now running back and forth in paradise—in heaven. Lord only knows, she would fit the bill of being the best angel heaven had to offer.

NATALIA

CHAPTER 27

❦ We all rose early the next morning, rushing back to the hospital. I didn't want to see Mother Gaines's body, but after being told that her wishes were to be cremated, I had to pay my final respects. The entire clan walked in, meeting up with the same Asian doctor we talked to the night before.

"Are we all ready?" he asked.

"Yes," we all said in unison.

"Okay, only three can go at a time."

First Lady sat down and said, "The three of you can go first. I will wait."

Pastor, Frank, and I all nodded, waiting for the doctor to lead the way. It was another long walk down an open hallway and then onto an elevator. Once we reached our floor, Pastor took a deep gasp, trying to walk steady.

"Right down this way." The doctor pointed.

We walked into a half-lit room. Mother Gaines laid on a gurney covered up to her neck with a half-smile. She looked darker than usual and her real hair was showing since they removed her wig. Her hair was thick and bushy, and her mouth remained cracked open from when her soul left her. I walked closer as Pastor stood in the doorway. I could only imagine how he felt.

"She was such a wise and faithful servant," he said softly under his breath, while tears rolled onto his suit jacket.

"She's in a better place," I said slowly.

We formed a tight huddle, sharing words of encouragement, tears, and pats on the back. Pastor quickly wiped his face and summoned us to prayer. He tried to get back to being dignified, but it didn't work as he broke down again, leaning against the wall. Frank and I stood on each side, grabbing his hands. He sniffled, giving us words of encouragement, although he was the one that needed it the most. He pulled back, holding the nape of his neck. He was no more good. Frank escorted him to a seat in the room and with weary eyes, he said, "Keep the faith, children. God knows what he's doing. His will, his way."

Rest in love, Mother Odessa Gaines. Rest in love.

PASTOR JONES

CHAPTER 28

ʳThe last forty-eight hours were gruesome. But, we had to prepare ourselves for what was to come. To know that Olivia spent months conducting a grand impersonation of a saved, changed, and dying woman was still baffling to me. We had no one to blame but ourselves, because the writing was on the wall. To know that she hung around during gatherings, holidays, and special occasions for evil intent was exasperating.

I went to Missy's room last night to see her, but she was knocked out cold, due to all the IV's attached and pain medications being thrust into her veins. I was hoping today she would be coherent enough to tell me what happened that dreadful day in the car with Olivia. I needed to funnel the information to the police. With Mother Gaines being dead, Olivia would go down for murder.

I trekked to her room alone. I needed this father and daughter moment, before allowing others to see her. I had piqued interest on her status. I stood over the bed, examining her body. Her one visible eye was shut and her hands were in front of her. Both hands were wrapped in elastic gauze. A black patch covered her right eye; there was a cast on one leg and traction pins stuck in the other. There were stitches going across her forehead, extending down her neck.

"Missy? Wake up, Missy. It's your daddy. Let me see those pretty eyes, gal."

She looked up, broken, confused, and misplaced. I sat beside her bed, reaching for her arm as the gorgeous little girl with a melodic voice I adored was not easy on the eyes at the moment. Her voice rattled when she tried to speak, sounding as if her chest was filled with phlegm and mucus.

"Hello, Daddy," she said with a half-smile.

"How you are feeling?"

"I've been better."

She nodded, blinking out water from her unpatched eye. "I'm ready to go home."

"Yes, I know you are. The doctor said you will be here for the next few weeks for occupational therapy and physical therapy."

She sighed. "How is Mother Smithfield and Mother Gaines holding up?"

I paused.

"Umm, Mother Gaines has gone home to be with the Lord,

sweetie."

I paused again.

Tears welled up heavily from her one eye. "It's all my fault, isn't it?"

"Don't do this to yourself, Missy. What happened that day?"

She sniffled. "Olivia hit her on the head with a gun."

I sat in silence.

"I lost control of the car and ended up in the woods. She escaped right before I hit a tree."

I rubbed my hands together. "I see."

"When will I have peace, Daddy? When?"

"Your peace starts right now, sweetheart. Just give it all to God."

It broke my heart to see her like this, but I tried my best to be strong for her sake and said, "Only God can give you peace, gal, but your earthly daddy will come back with your favorite candy, *Snickers*. Will that help kick start the process?"

She tried not to laugh but gave away a little giggle. "That would be nice, Daddy. You know I love Snickers."

I stood up, bending down to kiss her on the cheek. I had to rush out for a moment as I felt my strength betraying me, while grief slapped me on the back.

"I just wanted to see your face for a moment. I will see you in a few, gal. I got a lot of calls to make for Mother Gaines."

"Daddy, I love you."

I turned around, pivoting my feet and responding back, "I love you more, gal. Now, get some rest."

That did it for me. I couldn't escape in time. The tears came crashing down. I entered the hallway, walked a few steps, and broke down again, right in front of the nurse's station. I closed my eyes shut and when I opened them, Beanie Anderson stood in front of me. He held a dozen red and white roses in one hand with a big bag of Snickers Bites in the other.

We bumped hands, giving a silent greeting.

"Hello, Pastor."

"Hey there, son. So good to see you. How you been doing?"

"I'm making it."

"Good. I'm so happy to hear that. I've been worried about you."

"Well, it's not about me right now. How is Missy doing?"

"She's still with us, but she's in bad shape, son."

His forehead wrinkled. "How so? Is she alone?'

"She has a lot of broken parts and so forth. I will let her tell you about it. Yes, she's alone and awake."

He blew his breath out and dropped his shoulders in relief.

"Alright, I would love to see her. Are you okay with that?"

"Be my guest. I think she would love to see you too, Beanie." I winked.

I pointed to Missy's room and hugged him before he left my side. I nodded and turned away, giving him another look of confirmation that it was going to be okay.

"Father, I thank you," I whispered, walking out of the hospital and back to my car.

♥Missy needed him. The question was, did he need her too? Or was this just a *I'm paying my respects* visit? I prayed for unity. Despite their ongoing issues, Missy was now very different than what he used to know, and there was a good chance that now that she finished working on *herself*, she would take him back with open arms. *Hopefully*.

MISSY

CHAPTER 29

It was hard to lay still with so many different parts of my body aching and throbbing. My biggest advocate, Mother Gaines was gone. Teardrops was all I had left at the moment. I reached over to grab a tissue off the hospital nightstand. I heard the clanking of boots entering the room. I wiped my eyes clear and there he was...Mr. Goodbar, with his sleek raincoat, a Polo sweater, some khaki pants, and Timberland boots standing in the doorway. I had to blink again to make sure I wasn't seeing things.

"Hello, beautiful lady."

I didn't know what to say. I remained quiet.

Oh, God what was I supposed to say to this man? I gave him the floor to speak by raising my eyebrows for confirmation.

"I know it's been a while since we talked, but I got a call from Natalia a few days ago. After hearing what happened, I became worried sick about you."

I blinked several times, remaining mute.

"I'm so sorry things ended the way it did, Missy. I want you to know, I'd planned to come see you before this happened. Around three weeks ago, I realized what I walked away from and I was ready to come back *home*."

You can't be serious. After leaving me for a Halle Berry lookalike, now you want to come crawling back?

He licked his lips and continued, "I learned a lot of things while away, and I even went to Dr. Brown a few weeks ago myself to talk some of these things out. I realized I'm not perfect and I don't know why on earth I was expecting you to be."

You don't say.

I kept a straight face, meeting my one visible eye to his two.

He continued to volunteer information. "Yes, I know what you're thinking, and I must confess, I did try another relationship out of anger. I was so angry with you. I couldn't believe I moved here to be with you and you dumped me in front of a stranger. I was beyond hurt, Missy. I know it wasn't right to seek revenge, but that was the only power I had left to get back at you. You broke my heart."

I exhaled deeply.

"But, I'm sorry I allowed someone to fuel even more bad vibes between us. She was good for the ego only. I found out

205

quick that she wasn't the girl that God initially placed in my life. It was *you*. It was always *you*."

His eyes watered. He placed the flowers that trembled in his hands down on the nightstand next to me. He opened the bag of Snickers in silence, emptying a few pieces into my hands.

"Is this still your favorite?" He chuckled.

I ignored the question. He knew he had me at hello when he brought in the large bag of candy bites, but I had to play hard to get.

I winced. "Are you done?"

"Only if you tell me you accept my apology."

"I don't recall hearing an apology."

He swallowed hard as if his pride went down with his saliva, deep into his esophagus. "I apologize, Missy Rochelle Jones. I love you with all my heart and soul. I can't see myself with anyone else but you. I'm willing to be there for you until death do us part."

Um-hum.

I rolled my eyes, plopping a few more pieces of candy in my mouth.

"I know. I know you're giving me that look. But, I am so serious when I tell you, you mean the world to me and I don't want to be anywhere else but in your arms."

His words melted my heart fast as the candy melted in my

mouth. He touched the pit of my soul and he was looking so doggone good with his biceps poking and shoulders buffed. I didn't want to give in so easily, but the truth is, I missed him too. After all I had been through, I needed someone that could deal with my off and on issues. Starting over and opening to someone again wasn't my relationship goal. I learned a lot about myself realizing that I'd been a selfish brat all along, expecting him to do it all while I sat back, not lifting a finger. Dr. Brown clearly made it known that no man would stick around long with my attitude if I didn't get myself together. I was willing to now do my part, instead of standing around waiting for him to do it all.

• I changed, and the Lord set me free from some of my mess. Why? Because I finally gave it all to him, just like my daddy had always advised.

From what I heard, Beanie was standing there blinking his big brown eyes, saying he changed too. I knew early on he was my soul mate. But, due to my past experiences, I didn't know how to treat him like one...until now.

My lips curved. "Beanie, right now I need to focus on walking again. I have to stay here for therapy, so it may be a while before I can think all of this through." I reached back into the plastic bag. "But, in all honesty, I missed you too." My heart lurched to my feet. I gave up those words way too easily.

But, loving him was just that... *easy.*

He pressed down on his chest with his dark mocha hands, feeling relieved. "I will be here every step of the way, me lady."

His bright smile reflected off the bed post and my heart divided into small parts, covering each toe. His smile broke me down in so many ways, I couldn't help but to smile back. His tactic of reeling me back into his web worked completely.

"Okay," I said with a bashful grin.

"So, in between those bandages, do you still have on your engagement ring?"

I wish he didn't ask me that.

"No. Unfortunately, all rings on each hand were taken off with pliers. My hands were swollen up like balloons after losing control of the car and hitting a tree." I looked down, feeling bad about breaking the news of not having a ring that he spent part of his retirement savings on.

"As they say in Jamaica. Not a problem. Only a situation."

He slid into the chair beside me, feeling comfortable to stay a little longer. I gasped as he kissed me on my forehead, whispering in my ear, "I've missed you, sunshine, and as soon as this is all over, I will replace that ring with a bigger and better one. You *will* become Mrs. Anderson, soon and very soon."

MICHELLE

CHAPTER 30

One week later…

Mother Smithfield sat in Mother Gaines's designated seat inside Mt. Zion for hours weeping. Every now and again, she would rock back and forth, mumbling a few words under her breath. She had only been home for a few days from the hospital, yet looked ten years older than when I last saw her. Her beloved sister was gone and the devastating loss showed as she wore her emotion on her sleeves.

"My sweet Odessa," she mumbled to herself.

No matter how many comforting words, hugs, condolences, and prayers, Mother Smithfield's facial expression remained the same. She was withdrawn and the sheer audacity of her despair seeped into the atmosphere.

The silence in the room didn't help as I sat on the organ bench, staring at the urn that was placed on the podium. I couldn't believe we had to go through the heartache of death and the residue it left behind. It was easier to stare at an urn, than her actual body for most, except Mother Smithfield. A mere body or its ashes, either way one could assume Mother Smithfield would never be the same.

"How long has she been sitting there?" Pastor asked when he walked from the back passing the organ.

"It's been a few hours. She was sitting on the outside stairway, waiting for Deacon to unlock the doors when I arrived."

"We better get started. Play a few hymns as we wait for others to join us."

I gave a quick nod while placing my hands on the keys. Mother Agnes entered the church and sat beside Mother Smithfield. Her eyes were filled with sorrow. She loved Mother Gaines too. All of the mothers did. As I played "It is Well with my Soul," everyone sat with their hands gathered and their heads down. It was a small memorial service to honor and remember our sweet Mother Gaines, just like she would have wanted it.

"Let us all stand for a word of prayer," Pastor whispered into the mic.

Pastor Jones said a few more soothing words after the

prayer to the handful of people that gathered.

"Mother Gaines had a written request that stated we shouldn't stare upon her stiff body. She wanted us to remember her as the praiser that could out-praise David in the Bible."

The audience chuckled.

"We can't stay sad for long, church, because one thing is for sure, Mother Gaines made it to heaven."

"Amen."

"I bet she is shrugging them shoulders from side to side right next to The Father."

"Amen."

"Let us sit and remember her in all of her good times. Does anyone have any words they would like to share?"

Mother Smithfield pushed up on her cane and walked to the podium.

"Odessa and I were friends since our early childhood years and she taught me so much about God." She paused, holding back the tears. "When I first gave my life to Christ, she bought me my first study Bible and told me to never part from God's word. Everyone sitting here today knows I loved me some Odessa. I honestly don't know how I will make it without her." She rubbed her eyes. "However, let's all stand and give God some praise, just like Mother Gaines would do. She was a faithful praiser and even when we didn't want to give a praise,

she did it for us. Just stand and lift your hands up to God."
Everyone stood up, lifting their hands to the ceiling. Some
moaned, others cried, while others cried out to the Lord.

"As Odessa would say...Now don't you feel better,
church?" Mother Smithfield smiled walking slowly back to her
seat, yelling, "See you soon, *Odessa*! Until we meet again."

Pastor's face was drenched with affliction. He grabbed the
microphone and said, "Would anyone else like to give words?"
No one responded as he looked around the congregation.

He pulled out a piece of paper from his pocket and said,
"Although my daughter couldn't be here for this service, she
wanted me to read the letter that she wrote to Mother Gaines."
He pressed out the pieces of paper with his hands and said,

Dear Mother Odessa Gaines,

*I felt like going off into a tangent of remorse when I heard you left me.
However, I know you wouldn't have liked to see me react in such a manner.
You always told me to keep my style and sophistication at all times, so this
time I listened. You were the classiest lady I've ever met and you taught me
well through the years. You've not only coached me how to be a young lady,
but you also coached me along my Christian journey. It was your soft nudge
of encouragement that pushed me into greatness. Our long talks on the
phone, your kind words after every sermon, and your sweet spirit helped me*

in more ways than you will ever know. I will never forget you. Your presence on the front row Sunday after Sunday was volatile to building my confidence and growth. I will miss seeing your face and watching you praise God at a drop of a hat immensely.

I know you're still watching over me, cheering for me, and still praising God to the utmost. I strive to make it to heaven one day. And when I make it there, I will join you with your eternal praise. I will always love you, Mother.

Missy Rochelle Jones

‣ As Pastor Jones folded the letter, he threw his hand signal to play something upbeat. I played "Goin' Up Yonder," which has been a funeral theme song in most black churches.

The small crowd stood up and held hands as the song motioned this was the end of the memorial service. Pastor led the way as everyone followed behind him in preparation for the spreading of ashes ritual. When the crowd reached the water fountain, Pastor passed the urn around to members of the Gaines family that wanted to participate. What was left was shifted over to Mother Smithfield.

Within seconds, the ashes were sifted across the church yard. Mother Smithfield's emotions ruled as she grabbed her chest, exhaling deeply.

"My sister…she left me," she cried.

We all felt her pain and cried along with her.

Pastor gave final words. "Mother Odessa Gaines lived a good life but most importantly, she lived it with Jesus in her heart."

I stood back, taking it all in and moved by the sad faces.

Now being drug-free, I strived to be just like Mother one day…fully committed to Jesus Christ.

PASTOR JONES

CHAPTER 31

Two Months Later…

❦ It was time for rehearsal. I peeped through the doubled doors watching bridesmaids lock arms with groomsmen. They helped one another ensure every step, pause, and sway would be perfected for tomorrow's official wedding.

I pushed the doors open shouting, "Missy's home!"

The wedding party stopped dead in their tracks and cheered as we walked down the aisle like two celebrities. Natalia and Michelle ran up to Missy, giving a group hug and huddling around her. Shortly after, Beanie walked in holding her coat and hat.

"Oh, my goodness," Natalia said with surprise.

All eyes were on him as he walked closer like a rhinestone cowboy in an episode of *Gunsmoke*.

"I can't believe you're here. It's only been two months and you're already up on crutches?" Natalia exclaimed, looking

Missy up and down while hugging her in between words.

Missy smirked and said, "Like I always say, God is still performing miracles. Let the doctors tell it, I wasn't going to be walking until six more months of intense therapy. But God." She pointed to the ceiling.

"I guess your doctors don't know Jesus then," Michelle interjected.

"I know, right?" Missy said, reaching over, and hugging Michelle's neck with a long heartfelt embrace.

"Look at you, Beanie! So good to see you. You look like you've been going hard on the weightlifting," Frank said with enthusiasm, pulsing his arm muscle.

"Nah, bruh, just lifting Missy in and out of her hospital bed every day and taking her to therapy gave me all the muscle I ever needed." He laughed, looking over at Missy.

They gave each other the look. "Word? Alright now. God *is* performing miracles then." Frank chuckled. "You getting puffed up like that from just lifting her? Yeah, miracles, signs, and wonders for real."

"I wish I would have known you would be able to make the wedding. I would have ordered you a dress." Natalia sulked briefly.

Missy held onto Beanie tightly, with her other hand holding onto her crutch. "It's okay. Just to be here to see you walk down that aisle is enough for me, sis."

I interjected, "Maybe she can sing a song for the two of you tomorrow?"

"Yes! That sounds wonderful." Natalia ran over to the organ, grabbing the CD's that had all of her wedding songs recorded.

"I know you know most of these already. Pick one that best suits you. The program is already set, but we can adjust. This is going to be epic!" Natalia couldn't contain her joy as she jumped around, full of excitement. She was so excited to see her friend and I was even overly joyed to see all of them with smiles wrapped around their faces.

I looked around, enjoying all of the energy that floated from person to person. I was ready to officiate this wonderful ceremony of love and I was happy that everyone considered family filled the room in harmony.

PASTOR JONES

CHAPTER 32

The big day arrived…

The church was decorated with red and white flowers, white candles, and red and white bows on every other row. A unity candle and communion station were placed behind me. I walked inside from the side door with the groom. We stood in front of the shiny wooden altar, waiting for each member of the wedding party to come forth.

The ceremony started with the bridesmaids working the center aisle, wearing red and white dresses as the groomsmen complimented their satin dresses, with red and white ties laced inside black tuxedos, lagging them. Michelle was on the music keys, wearing a red dress that was like the bridesmaids'. Micah sat peacefully in Tonya's lap as his mother played that organ as if she was John P. Kee himself. She was all into it as the beautiful crowd of over six hundred people watched attentively.

I was having a proud pastor moment.

Seconds later, the tune "Here Comes the Bride" played, with the crowd standing up on their feet. The ushers dragged the bridal runner down the entire aisle before allowing the bride inside. When they reached the door, they gave the signal and the back doors of the church swung wide open. There she was in the flesh, Natalia, awaiting to unite with her groom once again. The justice of the peace had nothing on this eye-catching ornamentation called a wedding.

Tears filled the eyes of many watching as the bride froze for pictures. Deacon Freemon held his beloved daughter's arm as he accompanied her. Natalia's natural hair was blown out bone straight as the bronze hair color on the tips of her hair complimented her skin. The long and silky hair strands hung down to the middle of her back. Who knew that her natural puff tucked away all her long locks for all these years. Her makeup was flawless, and her eyelashes framed her sparkling eyes beautifully. She was America's bride, walking in with poise and grace. The hand that wrapped around her father's arm displayed a bouquet of red and white flowers. Frank stood beside me, watching her every move. He couldn't take his eyes off her.

She was beautiful.

His sisters looked over, giving him the thumbs-up as they

smiled widely as Natalia inched closer.

Natalia's white laced veil came down over her face, matching her laced, sweetheart-neckline-styled wedding dress. Her white laced open-toed shoes, with pearls covering the top looked as if they were over four inches tall.

She made it to the front, standing still as Missy stood up in the choir stand, grabbing the mic to sing her own rendition of, "The One He Kept for Me."

Only an angel could hit those notes and that she was, at the moment. She sung her heart out as her dear friend prepared to take her groom's hand. At the end of the song, I said, "Who gives this bride away?"

"I do!" Deacon Freemon screamed.

The crowd chuckled at the volume of his words.

"Dearly beloved, we are gathered here today for the holy matrimony of Frank Thomas and Natalia Freemon." I followed the minister's handbook for weddings, word for word. I told a joke every now and then and didn't miss a beat to ease the crowd as emotions flew from left to right. After exchanging communion, exchanging rings and repeating wedding vows, I ended with, "I now pronounce you husband and wife. You may kiss your bride."

Frank charged at her face, sucking her bottom lip with care. The music started again as the traditional wedding broomstick was laid across the floor.

"I now present to you…Mr. And Mrs. Frank Thomas."

They jumped the broom in unison, waving at the crowd. A happy occasion of unity, love, and hope for a positive union by two very special positive people.

It's days like this that remind me why I continue being part of *That Church Life*. It's days like this that gives another inkling of God's spirit to do what I'm called to do.

PASTOR JONES

CHAPTER 33

The entire wedding party filed out of the church. I sat and waited for the sanctuary to clear out, before proceeding to the dining hall for the reception.

Deacon Freemon walked up to me with an inquisitive look.

"Pastor?" He patted me on the shoulder.

"Yes, Deacon?"

"I need your approval on something before I go into the reception. I have something that I need to do in front of everyone."

I tugged at my beard, hoping Deacon didn't have something planned that would turn this love and happiness feeling into absolute agony.

"What is it?"

Sister Mary walked from the back and sat on the front row as his eyes gleamed back at her.

"Pastor, Sister Mary and I wanted to know something before I popped the question."

"What question are you pertaining to, sir?" I doubled back.

He gave a half-grin. "Pastor, when we enter into the reception before they crank up the music, I will be asking Sister Mary to marry me."

What the...?

I choked.

"Will you officiate our wedding?" he pleaded.

Deacon Freemon was ready to be a one-woman man and he was going to announce his change of heart at his daughter's wedding. I didn't know if I should grab the oil and pour it all down his back or shake him out of it. Cupid had gone wild.

"Don't let all this lovey-dovey stuff get you caught up, but if you are really serious…. you know I will, Deacon."

He smiled, grabbing Mary's hand.

"But, only if it is God's will."

He nodded.

"I 'm proud of you, Deacon."

We shook hands as we all walked downstairs together.

This wedding helped us to remove the sadness and treasure every moment together as a family. My soul was lifted, my burdens were light. God *fixed* it all. We made it once again through God's test. All is well. It's getting better, and the best is yet to come. *To God be all the glory.*

THE END...

EPILOGUE

It was deer hunting season in North Carolina as the male population flocked to the woods in search of sweet meat to add to their dinner table. A man and his son were hunting in a secluded forest, outside a small town called Bahama.

While in search of the prime Cervinae to shoot and drag to the back of their pickup truck, they noticed movement in the wooded area.

With surreptitious stares around the forest, a large object was spotted. There, next to a pile of rocks, sat a woman. Her torso leaned up against a tree and a trash bag sat beside her. She could've been mistaken for a possible wild animal, as her skin was blackened by the dirt she sat in.

The young boy shouted, "Dad, wait. Don't shoot. I think that's a human!"

The trigger-happy man inched over, poking the frail-looking woman with the edge of his rifle. She was barely breathing.

"Ma'am?"

Her eyes fluttered as she looked around, trying to maintain her bearing, startled by the shotgun poking in her side.

"What are you doing out here? This here is hunting grounds, and someone could've mistaken you for an animal. You better get up away from here before you get accidentally shot."

She spoke slowly with parched lips. "Where am I?"

The father and son team looked at each other in bewilderment.

"What's your name?"

She felt up and down her arms, looking confused. "I'm not sure."

"You don't know your name, Ma'am?" the young boy asked.

The woman scrunched her face, trying to remember. "No, I don't think so."

The father bent down to pick her up by her elbows, while the young boy searched her belongings for identification. "Ma'am, we need to get you to a hospital. Maybe they can help you remember."

———————

Days later, the unidentified woman was identified as Olivia Wallace. She sat up in a hospital bed, with soiled clothing piled up beside her. She still couldn't figure out what was going on.

She swirled to the edge of the hospital bed, trying desperately to trigger a memory. That wish defied the stronghold that over took her brain, but she was determined to figure it all out.

She sifted through her pockets redeeming a platinum gold card with a Visa logo. White letters stretched across the front with the following: *Pastor Henry Jones, Mt. Zion Holiness Church Inc.*

Suddenly, she shrieked, "I remember. I remember!"

A nurse rushed in to help. "Ma'am, what do you remember?"

Olivia scratched her head.

She masked a deep frown as her brain computed a name. Speaking softly, she blurted, "Missy?"

The nurse fluffed her pillows and said, "Who's Missy?"

She scratched her head again. "I don't know."

"I know I'm not supposed to be giving spiritual advice but pray about it. Do you remember how to pray?"

She nodded.

"Good. Just give it some time and God will help you remember."

Olivia Wallace leaned back, tucking the card in her hand back into her pocket. She pondered some more and chanted the name over and over again.

"Missy."

"Missy."

"Missy."

Missy...Who is she?

MESSAGE FROM THE AUTHOR

A big thank you to every reader that took time out to read this series. I am beyond honored to have so many people read my work, considering this series was my first of many.

For every person that loved, hated, and fought my characters inside your head, I thank you. I never planned on going past book one, but since I left a cliffhanger, I was advised to do so or else...lol. I love writing. It is truly a passion. My goal was not to make my characters stereotypical like in most church stories. My goal was to show the journey of getting to Christ. There is a journey, you know. Rome wasn't built in a day and neither was salvation.

For the one percent of folks who felt that God wasn't shown...he was shown through love, perseverance and hope throughout each chapter. Isn't he love? Isn't he hope? Doesn't he give us the strength to move and breathe through him? That's what I want to share with the world, the journey. As E.N. Joy once said, "We write about how Christians are today, not how they are supposed to be." She was right! Just because a person attends church Sunday after Sunday, doesn't mean they are yearning for eternal life. I will continue to write stories that make you think, encourage you, and pique your interest. As I put these funny and lovable characters to rest, I hope you are ready for the play or movie coming to a theater near you.

Love,
Teresa B.

ABOUT THE AUTHOR

Teresa B. Howell

Teresa B. Howell was raised in Boston, Massachusetts. She is an educator, mentor, and advocate for students with special needs. Born and raised in the church, it was fitting to tell her story in her unique style of writing. She currently resides in Durham, North Carolina with her husband and children.

That Church Life 1 & 2 is available on Amazon.com and Barnesandnoble.com.

For more information or updates:
www.teresabhowell.com

CPSIA information can be obtained
at www.ICGtesting.com
Printed in the USA
LVHW021533020119
602486LV00018B/1014/P

9 780997 773248